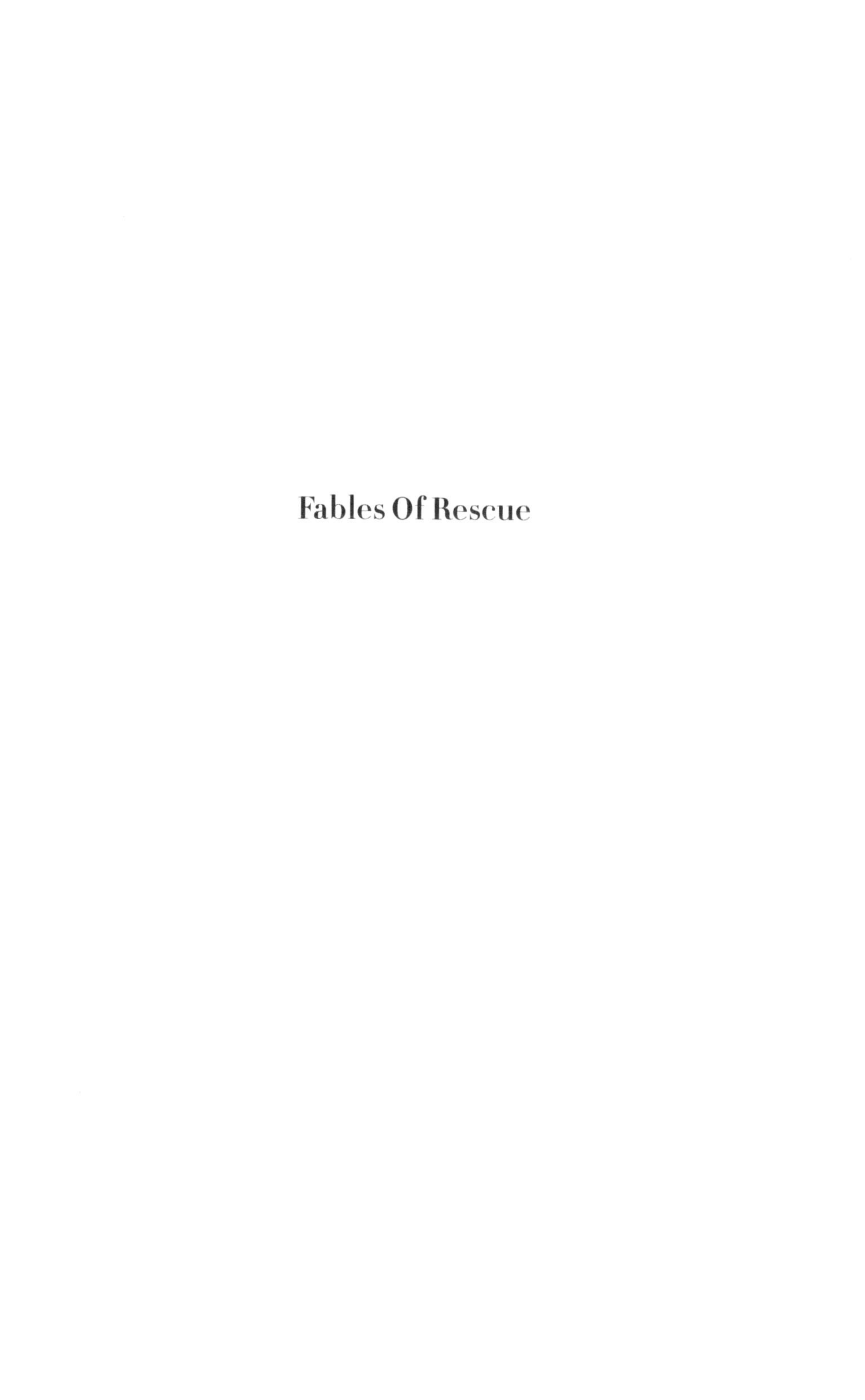

Fables Of Rescue

Fables Of Rescue

Stories

Richard Wirick

Ekstasis Editions

Cover Art: "Christ in the Storm on the Sea of Galilee," 1633. Oil on canvas. Stolen in 1990. From the Isabella Stewart Gardner Museum. Rembrandt van Rijn (Leyden, 1606 - 1669, Amsterdam)

Cover Design: Richard Olafson
Author photo: Heather Culp

Published in 2025 by:
Ekstasis Editions Canada Ltd.
Box 8474, Main Postal Outlet
Victoria, B.C. V8W 3S1

Ekstasis Editions
Box 571
Banff, Alberta T1L 1E3

LIBRARY AND ARCHIVES CANADA CATALOGUING IN PUBLICATION

TITLE: FABLES OF RESCUE : STORIES / RICHARD WIRICK.
NAMES: WIRICK, RICHARD, AUTHOR
DESCRIPTION: FIRST EDITION.
IDENTIFIERS: CANADIANA 20240459733 | ISBN 9781771715690 (SOFTCOVER) | ISBN 9781771715683 (HARDCOVER)
SUBJECTS: LCGFT: SHORT STORIES.
CLASSIFICATION: LCC PS3623.I75 F33 2025 | DDC 813/.6—DC23

What should we be without the sexual myth,
The human reverie or poem of death?

Castratos of moon-mash — Life consists
Of propositions about life. The human

Reverie is a solitude in which
We compose these propositions, torn by dreams,

By the terrible incantations of defeats
And by the fear that defeats and dreams are one.

The whole race is a poet that writes down
The eccentric propositions of its fate.

Wallace Stevens, "Men Made Out of Words"

At the bottom of everything is the Hallelujah.

Clarice Lispector

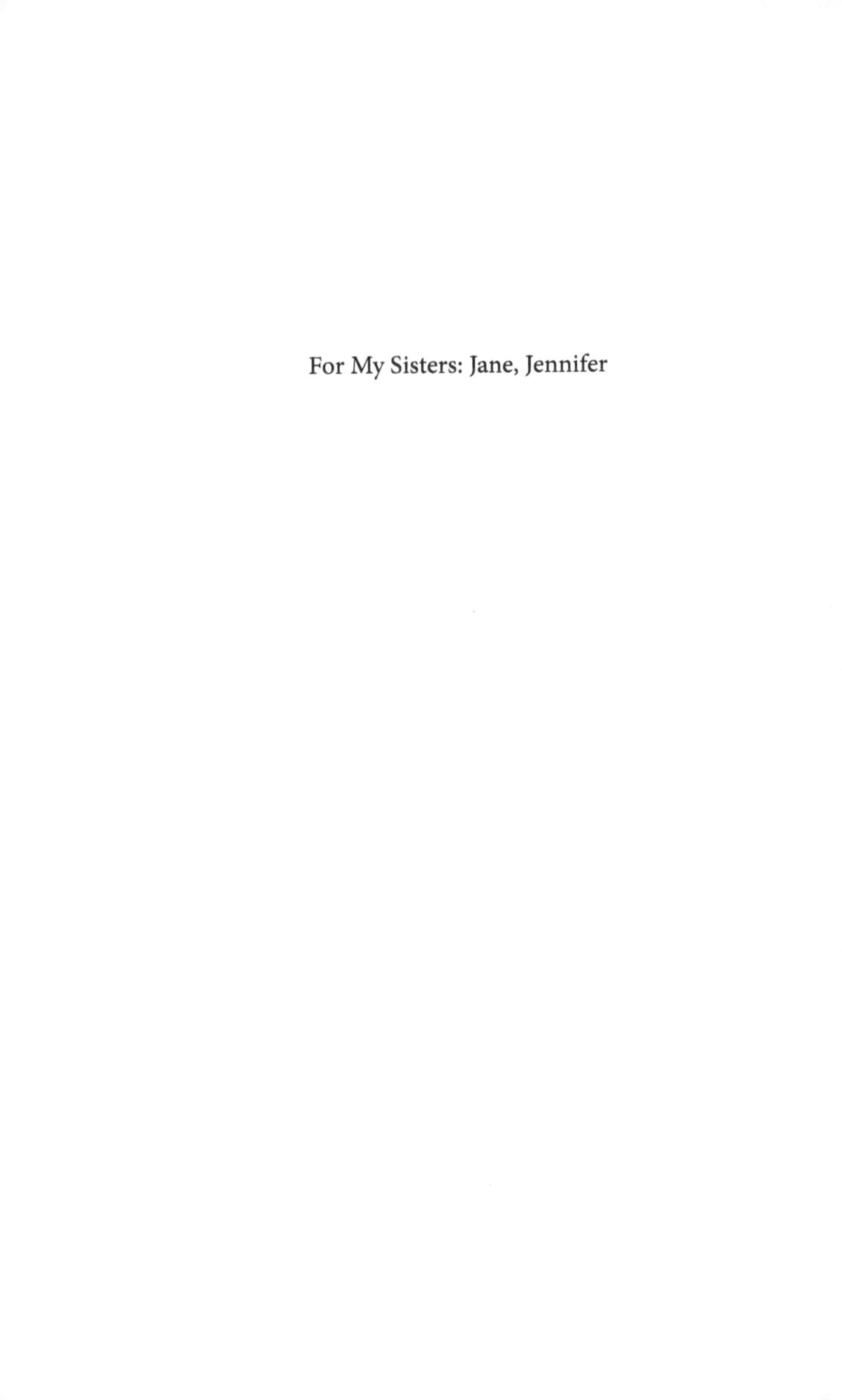

For My Sisters: Jane, Jennifer

Contents

Fables Of Rescue

Ophelia

Far out in the middle of the Lake, maybe halfway to Canada, to Thessalon, the wind blows the waves even higher than it does out over the open sea. Their tops of froth bend into whitened crystal in the frozen air, then crash like glass, thousands of broken windows falling into the unrisen water. Freighters, Jack knew, had gone down under their waves for two centuries, the crew waiting silently to die, curdling into ice themselves, in an instant, as the bow drilled down slowly and then much more quickly into oblivion.

"What the hell were they thinking?" his father said. *The Plain Dealer* was spread out over the breakfast table as Jack looked over his shoulder and saw pictures of the plane, a B-25, that the ROTC students had tricked out for skydiving and painted with an Indians logo on the tail fin.

The crew and passengers were in school at Case Western, aeronautical engineering students. Many were fraternity brothers, but some were women, girls really, girlfriends or ones wanting to be that so badly as to have done this. The details were being sorted out.

The plane had taken off from Burke Lakefront Airport, the new-built landing field for business jets that stretched along the

Cleveland waterfront like a dangling arm when seen from the air. The pilot had maybe fifty, maybe a hundred hours of flight time in a military rig like this. The investigation had only begun, the paper said. But the kid had gotten it off the ground, clicked the lights on with his hand console, and had correctly retracted the gear and leveled off at about six thousand feet.

What happened next was that the plane lost its coordinates, went over a cloud cover, and when the parachutists started jumping out into the winter night, each one bundled into a white down suit with twelve-inch body beacons, big as clocks, they thought they were over a group of football fields in the Elyria flatlands. This was the flight plan their thin captain had described to them.

But the plane had followed the shore westward without instruments, VFR only, and then turned north out over the lake and followed the island lights of Put-in-Bay that pointed not to Detroit but across the vast, dark inland sea to Ontario. When they went off the wire they were jumping into dense, boxlike cloudbanks packed against the miles of bridges and cargo inlets. Some were only a couple of hundred yards from the beach when they landed, but all of them drowned. The ones who hit chop water had floated ashore, bloated from days of drifting, their faces clustered with moon-bright hoar frost in the newspaper photographs.

The rest, maybe seven or eight, went down over water that was more shallow, that froze in the days after they entered its silence. They were still frozen, only a few feet under, and fire trucks went out each night with drills and floodlights to do the slow, grisly work of bringing the bodies up.

Jack wanted to go up and told his mother. She forbade it absolutely, which meant he'd have to make up something that Friday night about staying at the MacMorris's. Besides, his parents had fought that night, which always made escapes easier. His mother had come home smiling and weeping, with Jack's sister, the soccer player. His mother explained how the team, having never won against Fredericktown, put it through on a three-second penalty kick, causing the ecstatic coach to drop to his knees—crowd roaring—and propose to his girlfriend right there on the field. "The whole shebang," she said, still choking back tears. "He had the ring and everything, and her hands just flew up into the air."

"Women love that shit," his father said. "I'd have quit when I was ahead and got out when the gettin' was good. Now the man is positively bitched." His mother and sister immediately left for dinner at HoJos, leaving Jack and his father to fumble with TV dinners using the still novel phenomenon of a microwave oven. She'd really only walked out on him like this once before, when he monopolized the downstairs toilet as he sometimes did on weekend mornings, his labors taking him half an hour, forty-five minutes, getting through the entire Sunday *Plain Dealer*, The Sunday *Toledo Blade*, the twenty-four-section *Columbus Dispatch*, and sometimes even the weekend edition of the *Chicago Tribune*. He had always urinated with the door slightly ajar, but everything about number two was immensely secret and required a degree of planning that their mother could only compare to Normandy. If Jack and his sister made too much noise or dared to knock on the door, he would roar at them. "I'm trying to accomplish something in here," he would say. "For GODSAKE I'm trying to accomplish something."

After they were done burning their hands on the tinfoil, and his father had fallen asleep on the couch watching Bonanza, Jack went to Albers and bought two heavy-duty flashlights, the large yellow ones whose batteries looked like squares. He put a thermos and sandwiches in his old scout backpack and rode to the 71 ramp on his bicycle, chaining it to a tree behind the dairy signs. The trucker who picked him up was tobacco-stained, tobacco-smelling, the rest of the air of the cab filled with the odor of wet wool and piss. Far in the back, where the driver would sleep on long hauls, a dog yawned and sometimes opened its eyes when a pair of headlights approached.

The hitch was routine, like he liked them. No drunk or perverted drivers. Very little conversation. The ride was a magnet pointed forward, running along the rail-hard pull of his curiosity. He was off to inhabit the Underworld, to see what form the shades had assumed. He would move, unseen, among them, and then return to the world of the living.

* * *

The driver had let him out on Euclid, and Jack knew his way down the streets of East Harbor to what in summer was a long band of lee water, bright as a knife, stinging your eyes if you looked at it without sunglasses. Now it was piled with dirty snow and tire tracks, like a floodlit construction site. Out past the high beach lights he saw the tiny mounds of slush around the bodies that the trucks were still drilling for. Yellow police tape wound around the barrels they had set up to stop people from coming down. Jack hid behind a phone pole. When the rescue squad went into the long, thin coroner's truck for coffee, he dipped under the tape and crossed to the first of the squared-out worksites. He hadn't worn boots, or even shoes with cleated soles. He slipped and banged his knee, cursing silently, crawling on all fours until the pain faded and the night air, heavy with barge smoke and blown soot, began to bite.

He came up to a wall of ice, took a light out and switched it on. The mounds the drill had heaped up had their own strange patterns of melting—an ornate undercutting, like lace in a glass church altar. It had snowed lightly the night before and the new striations of white, their liquefaction and evaporation, had shown him how snow too rots at its own slow arctic pace, its ridges crawling with bubbles of meltwater and sand, suspended like dust motes in a shaft of light.

He was stalling. He knew he was stalling. He had only seen the dead in their coffins at family funerals, the ancient grandmothers made up with hats and odd perched glasses or lanyards of their Eastern Star, mothers of World War II and Korean sons. They smelled the same. The smell of the human dead, like old dresses, hung low in the air and entered the curtains until the banks of flowers crowded in with their reassuring, life-affirming perfumes.

But these were going to be, Jack knew, the real dead, the unadorned. The dead before hands would touch them and make them more as they were when they passed him on the street. Real people who fell to the ground in unthinkable terror, their last panicked look, twisting themselves up like inchworms on a trellis, lifting back from what they thought would be the welcoming ground. He thought of his own life now, a sort of sprung, uncoiled clock, his own, his incredibly own, that he must not let drop.

He leaned over and shone one of the lights into the open square. When he brushed away the snow the girl was looking sideways, her profile etched with a string of blood that ran from the top of her helmet down over her shoulders. Her hair was cut short. She'd been trying to close her eyes, but one shone honey yellow under the half-lid, like a bud splitting out of a rubbery bulb. One arm was under her, the other stretched out, pointing, reaching. Her limbs went in too many directions for their bones, all of them, not to be completely broken.

There were voices in the truck, coughing. A cigarette cough.

Jack crawled to the second square. He used both lights this time. It was another girl, looking almost like the first, maybe a twin. She had the same spun-sugar curls cut short and bending up out of a watch cap. She looked intact and dusty—as though she'd never hit water or ice, sleeping in a camp bunk the heedless sleep of the young—and out of her parka pocket had fallen three flattened cans of Strohs, the local beer, their tops pushed up against her side like nursing kittens. Around her was a circle of other broken, scattered gear, light lenses and pull rings. Jack remembered photos of long-dead bog women necklaced with the outlines of their own vertebrae.

Another dig was joined to hers, a coffin-angled shaft whose right end held the body of a man, face up, rigid with wonder at what he'd come to. There was a compass in one of his gloves. Jack read that falling people cling to objects, tightly, desperately, as if they were part of the solid thing they fell from or had looked back to, lastly, before deciding to let go. His eyes were sleeping, his lashes long as a woman's tipped with beads of perfect ice. But his neck was broken, much longer than it should have been and razored red like a bird's about to be butchered. Like a hanged man.

"Hey kid."

The voice sounded out of a megaphone, but the speaker was talking to somebody else and couldn't see Jack. He flattened himself, breathed slower with his mouth in a circle so his breath wouldn't cloud. "Back of the tape," the voice said again. But the man was looking to the east, up near the plank bridge that went out to the breakwater, where people had been chased—some arrested—in the preceding days.

The last one he could get to before having to crawl had the highest berms, but seemed the newest, its snow crisp-topped, untarnished. But it was high and freezing fast, and Jack had to gouge a dent in its side so he could mount both lights downward.

The girl looked as young as Jack, fourteen, and the ice was clear as a window she watched him from. She was a redhead, and there was no struggle or pain in her face, her eyes brimming up as though grateful, amazed. Like many of the northeast county Irish she had freckles. Her top suit snaps were open and the trail of brown dots swarmed fawnlike down her neck and into the ravaged parka. The lee water had to have been moving when she sank, her hair spinning on the surface in an orange circle and then, like a night-blooming flower, closing back on itself as the water hardened. He'd just read Ophelia's speech in Ackerman's class and he imagined her calling to him. *There's fennel for you, columbine. I was not wearier where I lay. Come live inside me, said the wasserfrau.*

Jack got up. She'd been a vision too much to take in. He imagined her alive, standing before him with her eyes closed, a little pulse in the lids, cheeks creaseless, smooth as a buckskin slipper, silky and mountain-scented. A bubble-gum tongue. Jack tasted blood in his mouth when he got up, and maybe his lips were that chapped and cracking. Or maybe his teeth just seeped this water of death, the final metallic taste of fatality.

"Son." There was a hand on his shoulder. He'd forgotten he had stood up and could be seen.

"This is a crime scene and we warned you twice." One deputy stood back a ways and shone the light straight into his face. The one who had tapped him pulled him up and reached for the handcuffs on his belt.

"Come on," Jack said. "I'm writing a story on this for the high school paper. Like everybody else."

"You, my friend, are a little shit. We told you twice to get back and you slithered around like a fuckin' grave robber."

Jack opened his mouth, preparing a plea. But the man was right. "Every one of you little fuckers, every night. It doesn't take much to fall into this shit and end up like one of these college boys." The deputy said the last two words with sour contempt. He had a tattoo on his arm, the Marine anchor and globe. Above it, in a fading half circle, was the word Da Nang in green-blue ink.

"We could throw you in the can but give us your parents' number and we'll let them pick you up. We've got a mobile unit phone and we can call right now. You sit over there and wait at the Amtrak stop. No fucking funny business."

The deputy with the long flashlight nodded. "You go to the vending machines? You get up and take a leak? We shoot you. Stuff you under the ice. Like we did that kid last night."

The first deputy lowered his voice. "Because you're wasting our time. Got it, Mr. Grave Robber?" He ran the nail of his thumb along the checkered stock of his revolver.

The Cleveland PD were bad enough, Jack knew. They'd been quick with the tear gas at demonstrations. But the Cuyahoga County Sheriffs were the dregs, PD aspirants who couldn't make it into the Academy. His father, usually kindly disposed to law enforcement, hated them, called them Barney Fifes. "Those boys," he said. "You fire a bullet through their head and it wouldn't hit a vital organ." He'd told Jack always to answer them "Yes, sir; No, sir."

Just then their captain came out of the coroner trailer and said the precinct jail was full and that people couldn't be left unwatched, and that people who'd been found out looking that night were being driven down to Summit County, to a holding cell in the big jail there converted from a Goodyear factory.

Not arrested. But it was where his mother would have to pick him up. Akron. The Rubber Bowl. The town of her birth.

Jack looked up at the sky, starless, empty of constellations, the patterns and names he had come to love. Something about the blackness of the lake and air, their indiscernible border, suddenly angered him—their broad unconscious strength, their serene unawareness of him, of the jumpers, of anyone. Farther out, beyond the bar, a freighter of ore cut north to Buffalo.

*   *   *

In the back of the sheriff's car he watched the lights of the interstate, the broadcast trucks coming up from the Columbus and Wheeling TV stations. The faces came back to him in a group, wide and light-colored as planets through a telescope—that same still, beauteous flatness, bright, unmoving in the melting tombs.

He felt, in that moment, that he would never die. And in the years that followed, when he was lifted into the air in the seat of a plane, he felt himself full of the fierce and reckless, fastened-together, together-dreaming and drunken jumpers. He imagined himself beside them in the starless dark, swaying, turning the canvas straps of the great chute's rudders, this way, that way. Maybe taking them, as they had taken themselves, to the end of the world. But maybe also, with just the right turns, this way, that way, steering them to some unseen, waiting island of safety, where they would drop and roll, jerk their harnesses and straps around the flattening chutes, and stand up, and open their eyes.

Mimesis

Marge's group of paintings came this close (Irene, her agent, told her, holding her finger a quarter inch from her thumb) to show space this year. But no room. Her group of landscape oils was beaten out by the post-post-structuralists; the dual post-conceptualist repertoire; the mobile hologram rotation that had taken Copenhagen and Amsterdam by storm. "The usual suck," her husband said on the phone, just before she, though agreeing, tut-tutted him. Brett was good to have close by, when he was in town.

Walking out of the gallery, up Ninth to their London Terrace duplex, Marge saw the same iconoclastic, genre-jumping works in the windows of the other Chelsea show spaces. The light of the winter evening sunk into the folds and edges of the empty boxes, the tumbleweed circles of wire, the fluorescent pipes and piles of seemingly randomly dumped objects in the show windows.

Setbacks like this made her post-mortem her oils, their sequence and selection, sometimes their very substance. What had fiery Clement Greenberg told her when she was his student at Cooper Union? It is all judgment, all intake, all immediacy. All how it strikes you, moves through you in the first ten seconds, leaving your opinion of the work forever unchanged. And tension, you wanted tension floating out of the canvas's surface, Rosenberg had told her. "It's all anxiety," he said, quoting Picasso on Cezanne. "What we see in the shifting planes of Cezanne is anxiety." The long inlets and sandbars of Montauk that she painted had the substance. But what she saw them lacking, why galleries couldn't spare space, was the strike, the ineffable hit on the line, that sense of necessity and exclusive comprehension that made the high bidder bring the thing into the boat.

This place, the place she was walking in, was the one place. The only place, the place that mattered. The three-square-mile nexus of Chelsea and Soho where all things, all movements and styles began and, if they had to end, ended in aesthetic quietude, a sort of sad and genteel grace, like the order of a soldier's funeral. The love of form, Marge said the Glück line to herself, was the love of endings. But there was no ending to landscape painting. So it had to have been the fault of logistics, presentation, her own or her agent's lack of aggressiveness and deftness.

When she got to her door, Costa the nanny was opening it to walk down the stoop to her basement apartment. Costa smiled, that "sweet smile of the helpless poor," and Marge returned the smile from her fastidious, frosty distance. Costa could see Marge's eyes were wet, and when she asked "*Està bien?*," Marge nodded affirmatively in that way that conveyed the opposite was true. Costa carried a stuffed bunny Marge had thrown in the twins' large trash box upstairs. They were five now, graduating to video games, and a week wouldn't pass without Marge sending old toys, old clothes and blankets, and paint-by-number pictures—truly hideous things, some of them—to their graves. She was puzzled by Costa's having the bunny, but assumed the trash box had overflowed and Costa was looking surreptitiously for a family-trash-verboten city receptacle.

Marge still had her head in her hands when Brett got home. He knew what had happened. He let his satchel drop on the wood floor and launched a crisp "Fuck" into the air. He crossed the room and massaged her shoulders. She hated this in bed, always the prelude to sex, but in these times of disappointment, of pure Platonic need, she relished the circles of warmth he made, the muscles up toward her neck unknotting in the warmth of his counterclockwise fingers.

"Call Irene," he said, surprising her, as he had always disliked her agent, who Marge knew was resentful of their wealth. Brett dismissed her as second rate, but Marge just thought Irene didn't work as hard for them—for her—as she did for the young, the fiery and hungry who had no fallbacks, no hedge fund spouses—people delusional enough to think there was a living to be made in all of this.

"You are tremendous," he said, one hand still on her shoulder, the other opening the fridge for gin. "Top of your class at the Union." She nodded as ice clicked down from the dispenser into the glasses.

"Tastes change. This place wants that and that place wants this. You'll find your platform. You are the twenty-first-century Claude Lorrain."

"But these are the galleries. Nothing important happens around them. Outside of them. I want my stuff in the row."

He sighed, taking a deep first drink.

"We'll be in the Caymans house in two days. Try some watercolors. J'aime Carib was made for watercolors. You should wrap up the big one you did on the Tobago sandbars."

"It's all so arbitrary," she said. "Yeah, they put all of Walcott, the poet, all his watercolors at Finley downtown, there by the Mercer. But it was because..." She took her glass and they clinked them. "It was because he was who he was. His textures were so flaccid, so repetitive." Brett came around and sat in the chair facing her. "We'll be in the islands. We can relax. The heat and the breeze will make you fruitful."

Their twins, five and full of the gods of war, were bouncing around upstairs. Costa only stayed on nights they had early Latin, and had locked her basement room and headed to the Bronx. She had three boys of her own.

"*Pinturas,*" Costa would say when she walked up behind Marge in her studio. The older woman loved her, pitied her, devoured the compliments while remaining convinced the nanny—herself from Santa Lucia—had the customary, expected judgmental deficits of the dispossessed. When people struggled to live, there was little free energy, too few hours to learn the mechanics of beauty. A Clement Greenberg line. "Mechanics."

She asked if Brett had talked to Costa about her accumulations down in her room. Nearly every stuffed animal and blanket and mechanical toy they had ever thrown out was there, running along the wall under larger blankets Costa had sewn together from somewhere else. Or maybe they had been theirs; they had thrown away so much.

A few weeks before, Marge had confronted Costa about it, but put it nicely: Wasn't it squeezing her out of space?

Costa said it was not, and that she would soon move all of it to another "space." When Marge asked her what she meant by that, Costa looked caught out, forced to stumble, and said simply "The Caretakers."

"Charities," Marge said.

"Yes Ma'am."

"Which one? Goodwill? Maybe a kids' consignment shop?"

"Yes Ma'am. The caretakers have many places. They do the work, I think, of God."

Marge smiled. This faith, she knew, came with the territory of the help. "He's too busy to do all the work He needs to," she added. Costa nodded at her observation, and Marge laughed.

"So," she said, "I'm glad you have it all sorted out for them. Tell me when you're ready, and we'll get a couple Uber vans to get them over to the place." Costa nodded. "…once you choose one."

Costa asked Marge if she had ever seen the women, the homeless women out on East 14th Street who couldn't get to shelters and who made piles of themselves—a single pile, really—over the grates and ducts that filled the curbs in front of the Con Ed building.

"I have," said Marge.

"They keep to each other warm." Costa cupped her hands together, expressing the closeness of their bodies.

"Is good to see," said Costa. "The hill they make there by themselves. At top, one woman. She sleeps, she says, with one eye open. She the guard. The watcher."

"Yes," said Marge. "The sentry."

Costa looked confused.

"Sentry," said Marge. "The guard. A word for guard."

"I see," said Costa. "She is like the Shepherd. Like Our Savior."

Marge nodded indulgently. Religion. That's where the artistic energy of these people went, dissipating, spreading like ether over the altars and brass missals and pews.

Marge was pleased with herself, completing this picture of a life she could summarize, could comprehend. She felt good to be helping Costa.

"She like the Mountain Queen," said the nanny. "The Mother of Our Lord. She stay on top of the pile. To give the light."

Marge was silent, the gin kicking in.

"Like a star," Costa said. Marge broke into another indulgent smile, reaching for the martini shaker.

"Like a star on a Christmas tree," said Marge. "Top of the heap. East 14th."

Costa gave a nod, pressed her hands together, and turned to leave.

* * *

The waves on their Cayman beach came in crisp white rolls, clean and even, folding under and into themselves along the strand all the way to Leviathan, the next town over. She was studying the lines of her landscape, one of the stranded oils, propped up on a tripoded easel on the flaking boards of the porch. The force of lines, her teachers had told her—Greenberg, Rosenberg—was the force of personality, the expression of personality's strength—the artist's mark of sameness and consistency. Strength of line also showed enthusiasm for the sense-data that occasioned it, making the work exceed its subjectivity.

The line on the canvas between water and sky was too strong. It displayed a doubt, an excessive burst of her own power. Conversely, it could be revealing her absence of strength, the weakness of her conviction as a craftsman. Holding the brush handle up, she eyed along the water's upper border. She could thumb scratch its edge up into the waiting air, but even that subtle a move could throw the balance off, bulge out or contract the system of planes.

The phone rang, Irene's number on the screen, and as soon as she clicked the speaker she said, "I think the bar needs some softening. The line is so strong it seems like a stand-alone structure."

"I wouldn't give it too much of a push," her agent said. "But you're basically right."

She could hear Irene take a hit on her cigarette.

"Any word," Marge ventured, against her better judgment, "on space schedules downtown? Next six months?"

"Honey," Irene said. "More like next year and a half. It'll be late '18 that I'd even be able to ask about."

Marge stared at the waves. She knew Irene was aggressive enough, that things simply were what they were.

"Margie?" Irene asked. She pronounced the "g" hard in her friend's name, one of those inside jokes of deep trust in a friendship.

Marge was silent, staring out at the sea. Her eyes filled with water, the same burning salt concoction as the great plain of blue, the surface that would cover everything someday—the found and the unfound, the given and the made.

The trip back was good. Brett kept up his broker's lingo. "You'll nail it," he said, leaning forward through the island's haze toward the outlines of the tiny airport. "You'll get the bar. You'll get the lines."

"You'll get the space," he finished, after her long silence, watching her finger guide him up into the rental garage. When he started to say something else her smile broadened and she covered his mouth. Pulling into the space, his words still hummed under her spread hand, something happy and busy. The sound of a hungry, hovering bee.

* * *

Two days later, having slept off the jet lag, Marge rose and went to her studio. In an act of cerebral determination that startled even herself, she quickly, very quickly, brushed the waterline's sharpness upwards into a softer border with the lighter, blue-grey, aqueous firmament. She sat down on her stool, enjoying the feeling of elation, of breakthrough. It felt chillingly satisfying, as if the strand's wavelets were spreading their coolness through the hot sand of her limbs. Victory was chill; failure was heat. (Who was it that wrote that the heat of Costa's peoples' homeland kept them so backward? It was not a racist but a climatological argument.)

So she was in a good mood when Costa asked her, standing reverently in the kitchen with her hands behind her back, her eyes on her espadrilles, if she could have the entire Saturday off in two weeks. One of Costa's boys, an asthmatic, needed a full day of pulmonary tests. "Just that day," said Costa. "No more."

"Of course you can," said Marge. "Is he OK? Can I help with anything?"

Costa waved her hand, sidling down into a kind of default curtsey. Marge knew the boy had an inhaler—these tin canisters were also things that Costa saved, piling them together into a Henri Bendel bag. Marge was genuinely worried about the boy, had helped her with co-payments before, and was relieved to hear from Costa that this new test was something the doctor had just learned at a convention, "to keep standard of care," his mother quizzically said.

Marge was surprised at the joy this permission gave her nanny. Whatever was going on with the kid was giving her a hopefulness that nothing in medicine, but perhaps something in her son himself, could possibly supply. Costa beamed one last time, turning around, walking, almost skipping down the echoing hall.

Costa wasn't really missed that Saturday. She usually came and stayed over as they were "date nights" for Marge and Brett. But Brett's suggestions for these had dwindled as the cloud of scrutiny over his office increased. There was talk of subpoenas, SEC investigations, people being forced to "lawyer up" before talking to anyone about any of the accounts. No matter, as Marge was ready to launch into a new oil that night. She would pour herself glasses of Chablis and turn up the Mozart. Sometimes she thought about substituting beer and country music. She dreamed, however timidly, of dipping, like an anthropologist in her own country, down into a world the opposite of her own: watercolors of the benighted, fly-over middle country—slag heaps and rusting bridges, toxic crutches of the heartland.

And there was something else that morning. She really would take Irene at her word. She could wait till the end of the next year to find her show slot. The assurance with which she'd changed the Montauk picture would let her finish two or three more pieces, get them to Irene, and progress would eventuate—leapfrogging from agent to scheduling manager to critic and to every collector that each of them knew. Funny how just one righted thing—that adumbrated waterline—could carry you over into some newfound country of confidence.

Gristedes was crowded for a hot summer Saturday. The heat had gotten to where the AC itself seemed a pathetic attempt at failed engineering. People would come in just to stand under its vents. She got everything she needed into a single bag and the papoose-like sling she threw over one shoulder and which had once accommodated both twins. As the checker stuffed her bags she saw the long line of a crowd waiting for gallery entrance. Something big was happening, the sidewalks crowded. When she walked out into the wet pillow of heated air that swatted her face, she walked just off the curb, in the street, to make good time around the sidewalk standers.

There was a gap in the line that let her see through the crowd. The gallery was one of the oldest and biggest, its front blocking the sun with a shimmering, swaying drape of fluted glass. Whatever pieces were being shown were structures, groups of them, about four to a room—the drape's translucence let her see just this. The structures had etched steel poster stands captioning the artist's work, and she was able to read them once she got the bags off her back and set solidly against a trash receptacle. As she was taking off the sling she saw something, small and unnerving, lying by itself a few yards from the first pile of "work." It was a balsa airplane someone had stepped on, or which had crashed into a wall so that its wings were flattened with the fuselage. It pointed to an enormous pile of brown and gray fur, blanketing, shag fabric piled on top of one another and woven through with glittering pastel boas and strands of bright yachting rope. It made a kind of fat-bottomed pyramid, and when she looked past the first one she could see three more conical piles surrounded by tiny ropes a foot off the ground.

She looked at the first description on the mounted signs. "Miss Enriquez," it said, "has brought to the world an art of the found, of the discarded." "The broken and abandoned are monuments to transience, to mutability," the mini-essay went on. "Ms. Enriquez has gathered objets trouvés and given the fact of their short lives—as toys, bedding, costumes, footwear—what the poet Robert Lowell called 'their living name.' Seldom has such vibrance and spectacle been found in such assemblies, but Ms. Enriquez has a gift of infallible selection, an uncanny grasp of the vitality of perfect placement. The critic Jed Perl called the Enriquez piles monuments to the aesthetics of comfort, of random retrieval and perfect arrangement. Her detritus gives us leave from our life, a kind of 'bliss of reprieve.' 'As such,' he wrote, 'her pyramids exude a clamorous shimmer, the fleeting and ephemeral gathered back into a new, beautiful permanence.'"

Marge looked up through the pile. Springed frames of small beds that had housed porpoises, bears and Raggedy Andys were lodged between heaps of flop-eared cows and soldiers and marsupials, all staring out at her with eyes she had somehow seen before, diffusely remembered.

Her eyes went to the next pile, pyramid, whatever the essay was calling them. There was mother sheep and her lambs, ripped and stained brown with food. There were whole intact tricycles, sleds, the plastic snakelike track of a model car course, its checkered flags drooping. There were pedal vehicles and plastic trees, covered by pieces of canvas and ripped serapes, cheap quilts whose edges faded away into a frayed, fluttering gossamer. All of the pyramids evened off at the top. Stuck into the third was the Bendel bag with asthma inhalers, the sack tilted sideways, the tubes spilling out and glimmering silver.

At the top of the fourth pile was a queen, an American Girl figure that a female playmate had broken while dragging it up to the third floor landing by Brett's office. On her head was a crown of tin foil, its spears smudged and bent but showing a diffident exaltation, a grubby transcendence. One of the queen's eyes was closed. But the other was open, watching. A sentry.

Marge forgot her packages, running out into the street in hopes of a breeze. The heat rose inside her skin like a blanket's warming coils, and when she leaned down to put her hands on her knees she saw it. The program, the same small essays. And by the word "Quotidian," finishing the title sentence that started with "Triumph of the…" was a photo of Costa, her Costa, her incredibly own, looking mildly startled as she looked up into the reporter's camera.

Property

In the city outside her house, there was a great emptiness. She spread her fingers along a fold in one of the brief's pages, then put it back in the row of ordered papers, the ink still wet from the printer, smearing some of the letters. She looked out the winter window to the first neighbor's house, a Turkish man who slavishly loved American culture and thus had nothing Islamic in the exterior except a tiny crescent and star above the door of a shed. An afterthought, like a birdhouse. Behind his house she saw the Merrills' simple salt box, expanding upward now into some kind of third story. The house behind that was a rising skeleton, its floors taking shape, the framers' work littered with the black and cream of starlings' droppings, undaunted.

Everybody was building, building. The entire town, the entire Panhandle all the way to Canada. The whole fucking countryside above Boise was sprouting houses, or filling the sturdy ones built decades ago with new adornments.

Every house contained within itself the seeds of its own financing, just as every work of art, she somewhere read, contained the very first sparks of its inspiration. It had been a hard road for her, getting a place like this in a town like this. Though her work at the firm showed promise, she couldn't wait for partnership to buy—the prices by then would be stratospheric. The money she borrowed from her mother and sister would be paid back. She'd gotten the best of the lot along this street, in this neighborhood. But the bankers—though newly loosened in their restrictions—had put her through hell. She could remember what she needed, and some of them were her clients, but she recalled a sense of rightness about the fact that Lenin had relished hanging them.

Down in the bushes in front of Arturk's house a gaggle of cardinals stood out in brazen scarlet against the snow. Darting and tagging, mating in fiery bundles, watching them made her think of Shakespeare's Leontes cursing what a bawdy planet it was. She had done alright in love. But the mommy track was death. And she still had time. But not now, not for that. The cage came first, the bird after. Or a bird with his own cage. The cages could be fused together, and hearts could somehow follow, somehow, with similar fusing.

And besides, there was something prideworthy and especially accomplished in the way she had done it, done so much of the closing herself. The climate of easy credit made the quicksilver acquisitions of others—those who hadn't suffered the front end of the lending chill—less accomplished. Less earned. Less real. This Protestant ethic presented herself to herself as a face of granite, looming over those smaller rocks that might scatter because their owners had no hand in the hard cobble. No hand in what had cohered. If there ever were a comeuppance, some mass financial conflagration, whatever else she suffered would not be a part of it.

The prior owner, one Jamison, had been an example of what bothered her. The price had been only slightly lower when she bought, and her meager broker's salary could not even have been two-thirds of Lily's. As far as Lily could tell Jamison's family had no money, she had no savings, no husband. What had she been thinking? What had Lloyds' Bank been thinking in giving her the run of a jumbo loan, shooting it through the whole process like shit through a goose? And she was younger than Lily—her credit couldn't possibly have compared.

And sure enough, Jamison had lost the place. Lily learned this from her new oracle, Helen, an owner from the other side of her house row who would come and peer quizzically at all of Lily's deliveries. She would crane her neck at bookshelves and stack units wheeling in on dollies, repairmen and painters, the endless parade of them huffing up Lily's crooked but solid stoop.

"She'd worked hard for everything," Helen said. "She wasn't about to let the bank take things back, even after she was laid off for a couple of months. Her partner's death didn't help. Living too large had something to do with it."

What had a lot to do with it, Lily internally countered, was sloppy lending and inflated income on her predecessor's papers. "Limited doc" loans they called them. She saw Helen as a dreadful busybody, not someone you wanted to share a shred of information with.

"But they did," said Helen. "She fought it till the very end. She got the Obama forbearance, and individual little pitiful favors from certain bank functionaries, but they knew they were coming for her." Once she got the summons, Helen said, Jamison became something out of a survivalist website. She boarded and padlocked the place from the inside, rushed out to rip notices off the door and uproot the bank's signs, and stacked up towers of bread and canned food like the crazed squatters in a CSI episode.

There was more Helen was holding back, leaning against a willow trunk and shaking her head. Lily didn't want to know it now, not yet. But deep down she returned to her own work in getting the place. An Obama loan! As liberal as she could be, Lily was sure she would never stoop to groveling, that thing they called "charity" in old television programs. If you couldn't make a payment you borrowed or raised the money from some place—one of those internet crowd-sourcers—or that was the end of it. Consequences would follow. Consequences should be accepted. You didn't go back to the lenders and get saddled with something mysterious and new. The reorganization of all the toxic loans—as much as the borrowings themselves—were what dragged, in Lily's mind, the world to a financial abyss at the close of the last decade.

Floor sanders were coming over on the weekend. Jamison had left the Bali hardwood stained and gouged like the craters of the moon. She hated her tendency to meddle with workmen, but knew she would. She put her Hawken gardening pants on a jacket hook in the hallway; the things were dirty enough to pass the Alaska test of standing by themselves.

Before the sanders came Lily had to wash and scrub the dust from other improvements off the board surfaces. And there were clods of mud from workmens' boots and rocks and wood shards stuck somehow, as if by some powerful adhesive, to the flat hardwood and its separating cracks.

Lily worked from eight a.m. till past eleven. She missed an entire day of briefing, but the sanders could only free up the coming Monday. Boise and all of central Idaho were in a remodeling frenzy; as prices rose, the smallest touch-ups, additions of seemingly useless rooms and spaces, added even more to upwardly spiraling values. Contractors were booked out months in advance, sometimes six. Lily had to get her own small shoulder to the wheel.

Nails and staples were the problem. They were the remnants of a carpet she was surprised Jamison hadn't simply left, like so many things, for Lily to do herself. The small metal nail heads and brass goal-post shaped staples—enormous things—would rip through her gloves: gardening gloves, leather or canvas work gloves, rubber gloves doubled or tripled up. The bigger the gloves the less nimble the claw of her hammer. She cried out if metal tore her flesh, but she bandaged it and moved on, relentless, with an eerie sense of owing it to her workmen.

At the end of it she lay spread-eagled on her back, extending her arms, as if making snow angels. She looked at the piles, breathing hard, gulping and expelling air and sweating like a marathon runner. The task had exhausted her, and after a glass of Chablis she passed out back on the floor, enfolded in one of its many speckled tarps. Water damage had come in through corners of the dining room and kitchen, probably from the bath upstairs, possibly from seasonal rains. Priming and painting them over took the next few days, and the next. Tiny gobs of whitewash clustered in her hair; she was too tired to return to the paint shop for a cap.

The painting came out well. Two glasses of Chablis, and this time a chair to sit in, regarding her handiwork, the fumes of the liquor warming her like the baseboard heat ducts which were one of the few things she didn't have to fix. She admired the way she'd worked around the wainscoting without tape. It had to be tidy. This mirrored everything in her life, her rage for neatness and order. A Capricorn, she feared disorder, which in turn bespoke the Capricorn's other great trepidation, which was poverty.

She nodded off again. The knock at the door wakened her, her dry wineglass dropping between her legs to the floor.

It was Helen, the royal busybody, holding a tiny umber pot with an orchid soaring up out of it. Lily groaned to herself, but a flower? Who, even in this congesting dung heap of a city, could refuse a welcome flower?

"So how goes the black hole?" she asked.

"Excuse me?"

"The house," said Helen, spreading her arms and giving a faux twirl. "They swallow everything, these money pits. So powerful nothing, not even light can escape. Except your pocketbook."

Lily assented with an eye roll. The woman was right. The list of repairs hung from a refrigerator magnet, four, maybe five post-its long. Plumbing issues in the guest half-bath. Dust clots in the HVAC. The transverse board on one step of a staircase needed replacing, but she could do that herself. But then she thought she could do the floor herself, and now felt like she could sleep for a week.

"Thank you!" she said, reaching out to take the orchid.

"Your wages for this devil's work. This man's work." They both laughed.

Once they were seated and Lily brought out tea, she stared straight at Helen, her chin resting on the ledge of her joined fingers.

"Tell me something," said Lily. "What happened with my predecessor? The survivalist Jamison? What ended up happening?"

"Oh," said Helen, "she battled them. It was World War III is what it was. She boarded every opening. She gouged out holes in the living room plaster. It was a battle royale."

"Where did she go? Section Eight? Did she negotiate? Try and suggest something, like a cramdown?"

Helen looked away. Her eyes had watered.

"How did she survive?"

"Survive," said Helen, stirring her tea. "She didn't, really. 'If I can't have it, nobody can' was her game. And she carried it right to the end. After sealing everything off, she tied some kind of pipe bomb to herself."

Helen looked away, then down. She poured herself another cup.

"But she wasn't using the right cookbook, or website, or however you learn such a thing. The smoke of the fuse she lit contained something terrible, something quite deadly. The bomb didn't explode. But she was poisoned by the primer fumes. Went into a coma."

The cardinals had come back to the Turk's yard. The women watched them in the snowy bush, two flames sparking and popping in the great circle of white.

"Never woke up," said Helen. "But at least the whole street didn't blow to kingdom come. It would, the fireman said, have taken out the entire block."

Lily stood up with a jerking motion, like a soldier coming to attention.

"That's sad," she said. "You know, Helen, I cannot thank you enough for the flower. I need to get going on a couple of things, and get down to Home Depot before the contractors crowd up the aisles. I hate to say this, but most of them smell bad."

This got a laugh out of Helen, and Lily laughed too. A perfect lift out of the dark place they had entered, a perfect set of goodbyes.

* * *

After the floormen left, Lily's tasks got larger, harder. The water heater needed replacing. She hated the way the dealer, a large butch woman, insisted on installing only the highest-priced tanks. "Otherwise," the woman said, "we open ourselves up to our own liability." Lily was too weary to haggle. A base had to be brought in for it, a canvas strap to anchor it to the wall in case of earthquake.

The list got longer. A crawlspace collapsed. Cement blocks came loose from footers, imperiling the dank, menacing basement she couldn't stand to enter. She needed insulation, wearying of the electric blankets and her heat-leaking roof being the only one in the neighborhood to not keep its snow. Bannisters creaked. She spent all of her weekends at construction wholesalers, filling grocery carts with astronomically priced gadgets and gallons of wood treatments, primers and finishing solutions, things she couldn't identify until their instructions were pulled out.

These were the weekends she used to spend at the firm, getting ahead of the litigation cycle, writing marketing and case development letters to keep her book of business robust. The dent in her "book" at first seemed the product of attrition at client's companies—bankers and insurers moved to other employers and didn't always take you with them.

But now she was losing more of them, losing them faster. Her department head asked if she could use another associate. She declined. Another company left her, then another. By the end of the year, when business portfolios were reviewed, the decline resulted in a loss of points and a good twenty percent of her salary.

Exhausted from the house repairs, she became jumpier, startled at noises, her temper flaring up at innocuous secretarial mistakes. Staff and colleagues avoided her. One client stuck with her, but its revenue-against-salary slot diminished. They explained they were trying to "spread the work around."

She remained a stickler on the formatting and style of briefs. But she was losing motions, small bench trials, arbitrations that even a very young associate could pull off. When she missed the deadline to appeal an opponent's summary judgment victory, she opened her client up to audits, perilous 10-K revelations, the search for another law firm. In January, the Capricorn month, she was called into the office of her managing partner and fired.

She fell behind on her mortgage payments, having had little time to visit headhunters or apply to less demanding commissioner's positions. She went into her savings, incurring penalties from retirement funds she would have cringed to ever think of touching.

The foreclosure notice arrived on a morning when she'd already been crying over a wine-heavy lunch, and her eyes blurred with a storm of tears as she read the chilly, anonymous death sentence. The sadness turned to fury. Where in the mail were the bailout solicitations? All those years of payments, interest only and leaving the entire terrible corpus untouched. The house was like a ship she'd gone from steering to having fallen from, over the railing and backwards down into a blazing race of black, quick water.

Section Eight! How was it those people, earning a quarter or a fifth of her salary, got to keep their mountain route bungalows? Why were taxpayers and hard earners, burners of midnight oil on critical appeals, tossed out to the curb at a single misfortune? Why did the squalid carry on with their squalor, being paid for it, while centurions like herself—the engines of the country's wealth machine—were left without any hope of second chances? Without a net to break the fall, without the lifting bounce of hope?

She refused to show up at the foreclosure hearings. She spent more and more time at the computer, searching with her lawyerly meticulousness sites she never heard of, never dreamed of going near. She scrolled through pictures of tin-foiled drug sheets, weapons, child pornography. The site she finally came to—all with black backgrounds—must not have been the one Jamison used. When she eventually assembled the device, tying it gently around her gunpowder and fertilizer-dusted neck, and sat in the recliner looking at the birds, it worked as promised by its goth, white-lettered instructions.

The Baby

Margaret was thinking about how to answer one of her interviewer's questions. She loathed giving interviews and loathed taking them even more, as she sometimes did for a quarterly to whose editor she owed a favor. Interviews, with their false enthusiasms and faked interest, reminded her of her prior career as a lawyer. It was like examining witnesses who lied to your face before going on to lie to judges and veniremen. Life could only contain so much dissembling. But here she was at it again.

An intern came forward and leaned down to whisper that her daughter had gone into labor. Margaret jumped in her chair slightly, apologized to her reporter, and unwound her collar mic as she folded the items on her lap into her bag.

Julie lived in Santa Fe, which always involved a layover out of New York. This time it was Kansas City, its golden tableland and drying rivers sending waves of heat up over the tarmac's confetti of sleeping and slowly moving planes. These peripheral cities were filled with smokers, and the smoking lounge, silent as it was with its TV broken, enabled her to get in a quick call to her daughter's husband Tom.

His voice was tired, as she expected. When she asked how they were he simply said "OK" or "Fine." Announcements interrupted the distant, disembodied voice. There was a tone beyond fatigue in his one-word answers. A spasm of heat climbed from her stomach up to her chest.

The smaller baby jet to Santa Fe was crowded with its usual Western hats, horse tack and bridles, and wet, bright orange garlands of chilis that looked like centipedes in the overhead bins. The flight attendants wore shorts. The old, unspoiled Santa Fe airport lifted her spirits with its carved oak benches, their cushions checkered with embroidered Pueblo suns and arrows and horses running away over hills.

Tom was gone when she got to the hospital. An orderly said he'd needed to go home to sleep. A nurse gave her booties and stood holding a paper towel while she washed her hands with stinging disinfectant. The orderly pointed down the hall. "Last room on the left. She's probably awake. She's been feeding her."

Margaret savored the moment she first saw them from the doorway. Julie was propped up in bed, her face red and puffy. The baby was asleep on her chest.

Margaret stepped toward them and Julie, trying to smile, only pursed her lips and lifted her eyebrows.

"She's deaf," said her daughter. "She's mute, they say. Her vocal chords were never really formed. Or they fused together. Something.

Margaret froze. She realized she was still smiling and shouldn't be. But she had to do something. She stepped forward and looked down on the baby's wet dark hair and perfect lips.

"She can't hear or make sounds," Julie said again, her voice breaking. "Did you hear what I said?"

Margaret closed her eyes and moved her head forward.
A yes.

"Does Tom know?" Margaret asked, leaning down closer, into the cloud of warmth and powder smell.

"Yes. He took off."

Margaret lifted her up and heard her daughter sucking in her breath and holding it, letting it out. When Julie took another, longer breath Margaret thought it was some kind of meditation or yoga, something one of the nurses had taught her.

"I don't know where he is," said Julie. Her mother held the bird-sized, almost weightless creature. She always marveled at the near nothingness of infants. They made her uneasy, truth be told. Was it Rilke who said there was no fragility like the human come down into the world? The grandmother (grandmother!) looked at the now blue open eyes, the smooth downy cheeks and red forehead creased by the womb journey. She loved the smells, the movement of its tiny pencil limbs. She saw the eyes looking at her, not quite seeing, the grown woman probably no more than a cloud of shadows and circles to the baby.

When Julie's gasps became a harsh, abbreviated sob, Margaret knew she was not rising to her daughter's needs, the moment's terrible, demanding uniqueness.

"Have you named her?"

"Yes."

"What?"

"Miranda," said Julie. She reached forward for a tissue out of a box.

"It's beautiful," Margaret said. *The Tempest.* But she knew she was being of no help, that her daughter needed something—something unnamable and maybe never to be known—that she could not give her. Julie wouldn't look up. The baby squirmed, and Margaret felt the deepest of shame that no words—that trove of signs she worked in—could come to her to make normal or joyful the place where the three of them were. She felt only a black, engulfing guilt at her failure, a desire to actually leave, which compounded into an even greater emptiness.

"She's beautiful," said Margaret, bringing her back to the new mother. Julie nodded. In a way that still could not acknowledge what she'd been told, Margaret asked if there were things she could get at the store.

There were. She made notes to herself and told Julie she would be right back.

*   *   *

Walking through the drugstore aisles, thinking of Miranda, Margaret realized that the moment she'd been through—it was finally sinking in—would be one of those junctures that changed everyone's life, that gave a new meaning to everything that had come before and after. There was no getting around it, no sidestepping its constant grip on the small, proud circle of minds that formed their family. The future would be a long, helpless stream of uncertainty, possibly panic—gripping and loosening, loosening and gripping again, slipping finally out of control like a car hydroplaning up off a storm-soaked road. What happened in the future would not so much be a continuation of life as an imitation of it, darkly congested, chocked with episodes of diminishment, of backward steps. Of stumbles.

She imagined holding the baby now. She had been sleeping in Julie's arms. There had been no opportunity for her to cry, to yawn with the small noises of wanting, of discomfort, the sounds of living and of rising life. Would she just arch back her head and try? How would she know, at first, what wasn't there in her, what others had but she did not? When there was something other than sight and movement in those that surrounded her, how would she be able to tell?

A bottle of something had fallen in front of her, probably only moments before. It was blue, thickly flowing out of the open wedge its container had become.

A voice rose loudly from a circle of girls she felt had been watching her.

"Margaret Stevens?" a girl asked, wide-eyed. Her hair stuck out in spikes. There was a neck tattoo, unreadable.

It didn't happen often. But it happened.

"Will you sign something for me?" another girl asked. She was opening a roll of masking tape, a white color, not the usual brown.

"I can put it in the book later," she said, looking for something she could lay it on that would not stick fast. "*Southern Bird* is one of my favorite novels."

Margaret looked down with gratitude.

"How long did it take?" another girl asked. The first fan was handing her the tape.

"You don't remember," Margaret said. "When it's that long ago."

She signed both strips. "Like it is a book I had once written, like someone else had written it."

The girls were sighing.

"But still myself," she said, smiling. "A different self." The girls laughed together, an anxious, giddy circle of mirth.

"It's really a thrill to meet you" said the third. She didn't reach for the tape. Her hero's just being there was enough.

"Such a pleasure to meet serious readers. Young readers. I never believe it when they say young people don't read any more." Margaret pointed down at the iPhones tucked in their jeans, and smiled. The girls laughed again, a feathery, almost-nothing sound.

No one said anything for a minute.

"I became a grandmother a few days ago. Just flew here to see her and I'm a little zonked."

The girls congratulated her in unison.

"I need to get some stuff," she said. When she said 'nappies,' unable to shake the word after decades in America, the girls stared blankly.

"It was such a pleasure to meet you," Margaret repeated. The third girl, who didn't want a signature, clapped silently. The other two, like twins whose speech was conjoined, said "Likewise."

Margaret walked on around them, her fingers moving in mock goodbye. The aisle in front of her was tidy and bright. She could not see where it ended.

The Branch

He loved being out with the old friends, the high school bandmates like Pasalich. What was it about it he liked? The memories. The atmospherics of memory. Learning guitar with revolving members of their band. Lying on the floor of Bob's house when his Dad was away, watching forms come into the ceiling as they went through the diminishing registers of chords, their recently changed voices changing into something lower, into the deep aquamarine of final harmony. And always the forms, the forms twisting in the popcorn plaster above them, the acid kicking in.

Both he and Pasalich were drug-sober now. But they weren't above dipping into his dad's bourbon or the cheap blended scotch the old man drank with his welding buddies. They nursed the heavy tumblers now in the late afternoons when Jack got out of the construction job his own father had gotten him.

So there was the nostalgia component, the valuing of a segment of life made holy simply by the stretch of time it occupied, 1967 to 1971. But Jack also relished how it deepened his detachment from a place he'd had to get out of whatever the cost, whatever the obstacles. And he had. He was the first in his family to eschew Ohio State in generations, a sophomore at Berkeley now. He returned home as an exotic, a perched watcher from a high place he felt he occupied with exile and, yes, with cunning. Silence too, for the time being. He deprecated what he was doing out West, partly to gild the mystery of his being there at all, partly because the philosophy major was proving so difficult.

The bourbon glasses in front of them fizzed in a hush of

bubbles. Peanut shells surrounded the bottle, and both of them pushed the scattered piles of them into bigger piles. There were deer heads mounted on the walls of the dining room. The liquor in Jack brightened the sparkle of the animals' eyes. Whose father here, in this town, didn't have heads of deer and moose and bear on the walls?

Later, instead of going to a bar whose well prices they couldn't even afford, they would make a "traveler" out of a thermos and choose a place like Swigarts, a fish joint that served Lake Erie pickerel, or a place even more primitive, a drive-in like Stewarts. They had gotten good at bringing the thermos out of hiding places behind a table post and filling the tall root beer float cups at knee level. They had gotten caught only once, and that was two summers ago.

Jack liked Stewarts. It had an interior you could sit in, its own kind of restaurant. They usually went for curb service, where both of them knew they could pull the traveler and see more action—the girls in their summer dresses, newly tanned and braless and full of the place's innocent credences, barbed with the devil's tail of dope. On some nights, Stewarts had a clientele of human swine, people who looked beaten up, turned inside out. We're talking, Jack thought, of human wreckage, guys with their heads on tables, eyes closed, vomit streaming out of their mouths. Women walked in with enormous hair and punched their fists into it, opened their fingers, made a puff like an exit wound on the sides of their heads. Jack was thinking it was time, maybe, to halt all human reproduction. But they decided to come the next night, curbside, top down, or top up to take the August rain.

The road from town out to Stewarts, which stood by the campground and reservoir bait houses, was wooded with a cave of gravel-whitened green. Jack liked Bob's old standard shift Mercury, still running as smooth as it had in high school. When he shifted, the crop of his hair still shot forward in the light of the dash dials, like a bumped mop.

When they got there they rolled their windows down halfway, waiting for one of the roller-skating waitresses. Single fathers had back seats full of antsy kids or, spoiling them, let them sit in front one at a time. Boys and girls came in pairs, no couples:

two boys in one car, two girls in another. There were elms above the cars, among the few still living after the blight. The boughs hung down almost level with their roofs.

One car had two girls, both beautiful, one in a sweater and one in a dirty letterman's jacket. Jack leaned his seat back, bringing the full splendor of the sweater girl into view. Her hair was luxuriantly blonde, its sides shining against the tanned, undulating sheets of her cheeks. Her eyes sparkled blue in the shaft of lamplight.

A lot of the girl-pairs got out of their cars, walked around and lit cigarettes. Not these two. They were enjoying the view, tapping their cigarette packs. They too leaned back, and the blonde lit up first.

They still stayed in the car, their cigarettes whirling, sending back food, peeking up over the windshield and back down at their plastic menus. But they stayed put. A breeze whipped up. They gathered their hair and straightened it behind their ears.

The blonde looked at Jack.

He was mortally shy for someone so good looking. He'd been turned down enough in high school—this very high school—and at college, which surprised and angered him even more. He'd done well for himself, but so much less than what he thought freedom from this place would provide.

He looked down at his lap, and when he looked back up her eyes were still there, glimmering, rolling with eager wet, fixed on him.

Jack got out and started walking toward their car, ignoring Bob's "Hey." He shook both their hands, the blonde's first, the other girl reaching her hand over with a competing smile. The blonde's name was Jill. He immediately forgot the other one's. Both had blankets on their laps, having been warned about the wind, this strange new breeze of the early summer.

She was a sophomore in the junior college, but wasn't studying a trade or one of the "pink smock" professions. It was, in fact, her second year of Classical Greek. Jack sat on the edge of her car, which gave with his weight, and he saw in the back the Chase and Phillips Greek grammar and, on loose sheets of paper, lines and lines of the stately language: Xenophon and Pindar, the beginner's snippets.

"Pindar," Jack said, "is strong stuff."

"He's dirty," she said, her teeth gleaming.

"Yes, definitely an adult dose."

She laughed. "College boy?"

"Yep."

"You down in Columbus?"

"No," he said. "Berkeley."

"Well, well," she said. "Lots of poets there."

"Too many," he laughed.

The breeze blew up, warm and strong, and she reached across the back seat for her purse. She brought it back, sat it on her lap and unlatched it, brought out a joint. He took it from her and raised it, nodding. She reached for his wrist and nodded him in.

"*In vino veritas*," she said. The white stick was straight up, an unlicked edge fluttering.

The brunette got out of the long front car seat. Its grimy, white and aqua bumps, like little inverted waves, left enough grit on her hands to make her wipe them on her jeans. She wobbled a little where she stood, but then stopped swaying. Bending down over the door, she reached inside the back and grabbed something, a cane or a stick that helped steady her walk as she moved toward the doors.

Jack lifted the car handle, nudged his tormentor down along the seat a foot, maybe less, and reached in his pocket for the box of matches they had given him at the cigar store.

The weed was sweet, paralyzing, the numbness traveling from the back of his neck to the moistness of his eye sockets. She took a deep hit, exhaling a straight stream. He took it back, sucked deeper, leaned against her. It was she who put her arm around him.

"*Pindaros einai endoxi. Endoxi, endoxi.*"

Her voice was deeper than from a distance.

She kissed him, traces of smoke still in their mouths. Her tongue was grainy, tasted of ice cream and root beer as well as the weed.

Jack felt he was falling. The seat was a cradle that would contain him.

The brunette was coming back.

"Latin sometime?" he said. "That old man Horace?"

They smoked for a while, but quickly, to finish before Rachel got back. She flicked the roach out the window, and pulled away and stared at him, happy, insouciant. She waited for the final kiss that he gave her, their lips folding over one another's like smooth deerskin, like fitted gloves. When he was opening the door to leave she slid back toward the wheel, which she came to quickly, her bare shoulder brushing the hardness underneath his pants. She closed her eyes. He closed the door. The sound of it was like a clock tick, that soft but that final, sealing off the whole preceding space of time.

When his eyes passed through the back seat, he saw the small, wooden shoe trees—or something like them—that you would see in footwear departments at higher-end stores like Linzmeier's. Other things were tangled around each other in the back—something like wheelie suitcases, bright and polished apparatuses, a silver appliance with a canvas strap.

She smiled at him as he walked away.

He had her number and her land address. In the next few days, he translated Horace in the afternoons, after long days unloading bags of clay from boxcars. He had never loved a blonde before. In the black of his own closed eyes, her two blue stones stared back at him from a ceaseless, tent-like golden circle. He imagined her conjugating the Latin, the low hum of it coming up from her happy lips. When he looked out to the woods from the factory railyard he thought of the Latin Silvae, meaning woods, meaning "a way," meaning, sometimes, a battlefield. Horace, sedentary and content, the old gray Latin Whitman, was the first of the Romans not to see heaven as the plains of war.

The images of her pushed his anxiety up a notch, smoothing it out into elation.

Through the rest of the week he talked less and was friendlier to people. He didn't seem to hear anything. He moved in a cone-like, silent space. Bob had to ask him things twice, three times, sometimes shouting to get an answer.

Meanwhile, and though she knew she'd see him before it arrived, she sent him a note thanking him for the Horace. There were Xs and Os before the single "J," closing, and under it a slim, descending swirl.

He would ask her out. The Malabar Inn, Louis Bromfield's cook's place, was still around from his parents' high school days.

They served river trout, pickerel. He'd taken his prom date there years before. There would be flowers and candles.

*　　　*　　　*

All the way out the highway that night Bob played the radio: Chicago, Van Morrison, the low-voiced Jim Morrison and the even lower-voiced Cleveland FM rock DJ. Jack kept muttering Latin, sometimes out loud, but the sound of it was buried under the radio's blare, the tires' flabby, hissing grip on the gravel. He had her note in his pocket. She had given him her number, but realized only now that he'd never called her.

The girls were in the same space as always. Bob pulled the Mercury in, and Jack could see that she was already looking in his direction. He turned to her, sitting on the passenger's side, and she waved.

He worked out the words of the way he would ask her out. Horace was the poet of stasis, of calm. It gave him something to cloak the inn pitch in—settled evenings, a day's work behind them both. No plans. Glass after glass of wine as the verses flowed.

How could he not pull this off? It was the Seventies. There were no rules of asking any more. Still, he needed to work up the moxie. He let the anxiety mount up under him, climbing up on top of it to ride it like a wave.

She'd gotten a milkshake and was pulling the sweet white of it up through the straw, watching him, smiling. Rachel was sleeping at the wheel. Maybe they'd drunk somewhere or toked up to ready themselves for this place, this palace of druggy hunger.

One foot in front of the other, he said to himself. It was a Mark Strand poem he used to summon courage before answering a question from his profs. He stood up and got out. But his hand was frozen on the door handle. There was no thought without language, he knew, which made these metered invocations all the more effective. *One foot in front of the other/That is the way I do it.*

Jill stared at him. What was it? Her movements up to this point, like those on most nights, were languorous. But he could see a brimming energy reddening her skin. She was bent on doing something. He could tell from the way she looked toward the sky.

She tossed off the scarf from her shoulders and reached up toward the low hickory branch not two feet above the rim of their windshield. Her white, red-nailed hands wrapped themselves around the bark.

She lifted herself.

She was completely above the car seat now, free enough to swing back and forth. But below the short skirt she wore there was no more of her. Her body simply did not continue. There were no legs. No feet or shoes. He looked to where her calves and knees should have been and there was only air, only the branches of the shrub fence swaying in the haze on the other side of the car.

She let go of the bough by spreading her hands, as if waving or signaling to someone. She landed hard, dropping with a whump in the passenger's seat. Rachel wakened, and Jill looked over at him, wiping the bark chips off of her hands. Her face was expressionless, calm. It showed absolutely nothing.

His heart began its breathless, steadily rising pulsing, burning in hot circuits along the inside of his chest and shoulders. It was purely fright, he knew, at what she was. And along with it, like a sickly bass note holding its jagged rhythm, was his judgement of himself, something akin to hatred, at knowing nothing would come of this, of any of it.

How could he not go over to her after such knowledge, such revelation? But he didn't. He wouldn't. He sat frozen in his seat, numb, imagining what it must have been like in ancient days to be the witness of some prophecy. The neon curve of lights blinked stupidly, on and off around the drive-in canopy. He stared straight ahead, his hands on the wheel at ten and two o'clock, like you were supposed to when the cops stopped you and you were carrying something they must never, ever find.

Tyumen Is My Dwelling Place

There was another incident with my Uncle Dmitri. As before, it involved his trying to come for Sunday supper, and my mother keeping him from coming inside, and his waiting for some time before getting back in his car and driving back to Moscow again. These times are painful, but they are a test of us. *Lo are the tested the true vine, it is written; only the tempest of wickedness sures the binding of their troth.*

We live in the city of Tyumen, here in the most removed and earliest-settled places east of the Urals. The great main river of the same name flows through here, and each of its five branches flows through each of the five adjoining towns and out into the Obskaya Gulf. All the rivers' names come from the native Siberian tribes, who we learned from Patriarch Yoshkar were the very sons of the original Tribes of Cain. Their languages were beautiful, he said, but their savagery caused them to turn aside the olive branch of our forefathers, the White Russian settlers, and lose forever the chance of redemption our ancestors offered them.

We ourselves are Orthodox, from the Eastern Church in what was once Byzantium. We believe the Scriptures are the actual and unmediated Word of God. We believe it is *the Truth of His mouth as He has chosen to constitute and deliver it through the earthly vessels of His Prophets.* We believe he has *lifted all veils, and where he has not has fitted the figure of nature to make his Revelations plain.*

I am eighteen, the last of three girls. There are twelve of us living here in our three houses, but I am the only one of this age: too old for school but too young to leave home yet, waiting to see which way in the world I am pointed to go. I have two sisters with husbands and children still in the earlier grades. I was born late. A gift, my father said. Dmitri is my mother's only sibling, the only brother. My father was an only child, so Dmitri is in fact the only other relation we have inside that generation.

My father is an old-style Soviet father, a stonemason, a valuable trade. Without him and those of his craft, there would be no building, *no dwelling rising up from the waste of the plain.* He is a tall man, his arms large with the strength of his building. His eyes are flat and gray as the mortar he cleaves the stone with, and though he smiles, the corners of his mouth turn down at the same time, strangely, with the steady tap and scrape and wiping trowel of his authority. It is happiness like the Lord's own happiness, one that is *filled with the work ahead and hence will have no truck with nonsense.* It is happiness, but a happiness without laughter.

My mother is a cripple. Even so, her nature is more gay than his. She walks with one crutch only. She does not lean on it, but swings it around and pulls herself forward to the place where she has planted it. Her eyes are blue, bright blue as bellflowers, and her hair is yellow-bright as the corn that has withered young and will never harden and change.

She takes the edge off his cold steel, she says, and this is the way things are on the day of Dmitri's visits.

For hours before Dmitri comes, my father goes on and on about Moscow. Moscow is Sodom, he says. It is a City of the Plain as festering as the cities written of in the accounts of the prophets. No good grows there, he will mutter. He says it from under the Pravda that's open in front of his face.

Mother's eyes look at mine as we work, bright bellflower blue, and I want her to sometimes raise them at me in some kind of small complicity. But this she will not do. She looks down when her eyes meet mine, and she shakes her head. The problem of Dmitri is hardest by far for her, as he is the baby brother she mothered as much as her own mother favored her, and sees now in her later years what has come of that, of raising him up among an absence of men.

It will take Dmitri a good thirteen hours to drive here. It

would only be half a day on a good road, but the roads to these back places are unpaved and potted, and some still have one-lane bridges over the five rivers.

I see him setting out from his apartment—a townhouse, it is called—right now, after walking his tiny dog and setting the alarm with the keypad on the wall. Dmitri is always well-groomed, like all of his friends, all men. He is clean and good-smelling, bright as a kopeck. I watched him lock the door like this once, and when he put the key in his pocket I could see the heavy ID bracelet fall down and glint on his wrist.

Dmitri has neighbors in Moscow. His neighbors. All young men and professors like him, and students. They seem happy, full of their music and learning. What is that if not fraternity? It is their fraternity. They laugh loudly, shaking the ice in their drinks and mock-punching one another. Some even go to church. To churches filled with others like them, men linked together with other men. My father and my brothers-in-law argue about the mason guilds and scripture in the same conversation. *This is how our faith is lived*, I've heard him say. There is no separation of the supernatural from the natural.

When I am at Dmitri's, the world here feels like it is the opposite of him. Opposed and parallel, like Dr. Klebem says in chemistry class, the magnets whipping each other away from their force fields, gathering the flower shapes of the iron filings around themselves. I believe that I would flourish there, in Moscow, like a rose in the meadow grasses. My faith would not falter but would give me strength, the very strength that everyone here is constantly talking about. It would be as if I lived in another country. I could live, I know, among other people as certainly as I live here now, even if I did not know their language. I see myself in a restaurant, running my finger down the lines of the menu with my eyes closed. At the instant I open them I say a passage out of Corinthians, and where my finger has stopped I will know the Words.

My sister Sveta is staring at me. Her face is plain, like the women in photographs of the Great Patriotic War, with all their beauty and desire burned away and bleached down into a brown monotone. But she loves me. This I know. I see it in the steadiness of her hands tossing up the cut tips of the blood-red peppers and vegetables.

She, like Irina, who is two years her elder, is the true breadwinner of her family. Sveta works full time as the church secretary. Her husband Zeb, or Zebulon, preserves old threshing machines and tractors for the farmers here.

But it is not a steady occupation, and vodka has been known to take him away for a time.

My father passes food to Zeb, who passes it to Irina and her husband Georgi. Father and Georgi agree that Solzhenitsyn is a huckster and embodies the worst traits of evangelism. When they tell jokes about the great writer, my father makes the kind of smile of which he is capable, the expression that is grimacing and lean.

I hear the wheels of Dmitri's car in the driveway.

The sound of the door of a car like his is soft, a cluck, like someone clucking their tongue in their mouth. His steps are a long time on the gravel, tiny crunches in the stones, and then they are on the boards of the porch. My father raises his hand in the half-second before the knock, as though he could tell the precise instant when it would come. My mother gets up, the beginnings of a flash of defiance on her face. But she knows even as she is making it that she will not cross him. She walks not to the door, even though there is a second knock, but to the oven, where something that is baking needs to be tended to.

Under the cover of her movements, I can lean back and see Dmitri through the blinds, standing and shifting with his hands in his pockets. I cannot see his head. He is wearing khaki pants and a tight, form-fitting maroon sweater under his black leather coat. The ID bracelet glimmers in the sun, hanging heavy on his graceful wrist.

"Leave it," says father. He is talking about the cake and Dmitri both. My mother paces back and forth now in the shaft of sunlight.

"Leave it," my father says again. His hand is still hanging in the air. "Don't answer."

The burning feeling has spread to the tips of my fingers and toes and into my hair now, it seems. I imagine it in the hollows of my bones. It is the power, I imagine, that some mothers have when they are able to lift cars up off their children. *What strengths come from a righteous fury. What lay upon the face of the earth hath traveled, even from out of its darkling core.*

Dmitri has never knocked a third time. He has once or twice walked to the window whose blinds are bent enough for him to think he can see in, but nothing is seen by either him or us. This time he does nothing. He walks back to the car, through the gravel noises and the door's cluck and the sudden awakening of the expensive engine's hum, everything reversing.

Not long ago I had a dream of Dmitri. We were looking at one another through a great porch screen. It was either the big one that wraps around the Moscow apartment or the one right here, the one he knocked on today and that stands not four feet from me now as I write this.

The barrier it amounts to had begun to dissolve. It faded and blended with the sky behind it so that our hands could pass to one another's. My fingers kept going past his open palm, reaching in between his ribs as I imagine God's hand had reached into Adam's.

For a moment, joined together as we were, I felt as though I had come to a place prepared for us like the banquet table in the psalm, a place of shelter in the presence of our enemies. A made place, a place of first permission. We could be there spirit to spirit, as one spirit and as we had been in the briefness of the moments at his house parties, or when our eyes would meet across the sea of heads in the cool dark of Belorussia Station. Spirit to spirit. Bright center of heaven.

But it is only a dream, and I knew as the power drained out of me that it had to remain such. To hear the knock is glorious. To hear the knock could be one's heart's desire. But to open the door and actually go out—that is something different. That is something else entirely.

Green, Whale-Back Mountain

The phone woke him up. He heard the greeting, and then heard a deep, accented voice crackling from across the river in West Virginia. It seemed now that was where the calls always came from.

"Your advertisement. The Kohans. We will come to arrive at four o'clock."

He pulled himself up and looked out the window. The Appalachian foothills were filled with morning sunshine. Great bands of shade grew through their hollows, a slow but still moving darkness that he had always imagined to be the only visible movement of time. These small green mountains ran the length of Hocking county, holding the river of the same name that swelled with rain and raced away East into the silent, brown Ohio—the river they called Leviathan—at the towns of Belpre and New Willow Temple.

He looked at their mailbox across the road. "Haroupia" it said. The final "n" was hidden by an elderberry branch.

"Approximately," the phone message went on. "To four o'clock."

Philip's stomach turned at the sound of the voice signing off with a "Thank you." It was the same accent, the accent of the Hoowan people that had come the last time to buy one of their horses and who had seemed at first like any of the other buyers who traveled in from the small towns around Parkersburg, the sprawling and hazy city on the River's other side. His father had told him about the Hoowan. They were hill tribes from a country over near Viet Nam, though his father had never seen them when he was fighting the war there. They were traders, shopkeepers, farmers. There had been stories about them in the Cincinnati and Athens papers. They had struggled to leave the country whose government had grown up around their ancient villages, and whose army had chased them out through mountains much like these, shooting men, mothers, even children in the back as they ran.

The other Hoowan family had come only a month ago with a borrowed horse trailer without a top. The car they drove was nice enough. After Philip's father and the man had done the paperwork and the barn hand had marched the horse up the plank, it seemed as normal as any other sale.

Then the father had started to get in the driver's side but brought something out of the cab. Before Philip and his father and mother and his sister could do anything, before any of them could even think, the man lifted a rifle to the horse's head and pulled the trigger. The animal dropped down in a great spray of blood. The trailer bed sagged as if a load of rocks had been poured into it.

His mother and 'Irin had run screaming into the house, and Philip had crouched when he heard the shot. The man got in the truck and drove away quickly. His father called animal control, and two officers came out to make a report.

It was then that they learned that the Hoowan killed horses for meat, or at least had eaten them back in their native land. There was nothing anybody could do now because the Hoowan man had paid for the horse. It was his property. The officers made his father sign the sheet on the clipboard and separated out a yellow copy and handed it to him.

In the days and weeks that followed, there was little talk about what had happened. It was mentioned in a tiny box story in the Athens paper, stating that the man had been cited for discharging a firearm on someone else's property. Philip's mother decided the time might be right to go with 'Irin to see relatives in Armenia; they had not been there since the earthquake in 1986. His father had cleaned the horse's skull and brain fragments from the corral posts. In the ghostly kind of non-speech that families talk in around the house and dinner table, it became understood—at least by Philip—that no more horses would be sold to anybody south river.

In the barn his father built after making what he called the "big money" in construction, Philip looked down on the horses each day from his perch in the feedstalls. The older man wandered on ahead, speaking to the animals in the snappy salesman's speech he had learned from his father, the first to live in America. Philip simply watched the great brown chewing heads, waiting for them to throw their mouths in the air when he re-filled their buckets of oats.

In the shop corner of the barn Philip found a mower blade his father had stuffed in a box to go to the dump. Philip picked it out, and for no reason he could think of other than the sadness he still felt at such a large animal's death, he began wrapping one end of the blade with adhesive tape, sticky and soft, white and thick and hanging with threads. Later he brought it upstairs to his room. It went under some loose ash floorboards his mother had not yet discovered.

As summer was ending, his mother's postcards stacked up on his desk, Philip suspected his father would try to sell horses again, though the boy figured he would be more careful. Philip almost had a premonition about new ads the man might place, new rumors he would be spreading through the feed stores and lumberyards. Philip felt his father's horror at what they had witnessed together as deeply as his own, as a sort of different note in his family's single chord of grief. If he could put a sound to his own feelings, it would be harsher than his father's: the crack and stretch of tape ripping off a roll, being wound around and around the swing blade's handle.

But Philip was also, he thought, uncovering something about the will of the Haroupian men. Horse trading was what his father did now that he was retired, and he would have to get back in the game sooner or later. His father only knew by doing. "Action is the machinery of faith." The Armenian proverb was quoted to him and his sister until they learned to roll their eyes, and then it was recited to them even more.

Doing, not thinking so much, was the way the man learned and tried to teach them all to learn. Surely thinking things through from every direction lessened the chances of error. But sometimes just getting up and moving, moving could do it too, his father would say. For him just opening the door wider chased the waiting mistakes away, the sun sending the rats back into the hay.

His father had given him the morning off and the two of them knew what was in the works. When the truck came up their road he saw a man with a moustache driving. Next to him was a six or seven-year-old boy. An older son, thin and very tall, stood at the rail sides of the plain flatbed trailer. The breeze blew his tattered Bengals T-shirt against his chest.

Philip was relieved of even having to entertain the boys. The barn hands would take them into the kitchen and give them lemonade and cookies. Philip stayed up in his room. He had taken the swing blade out. He folded his hand into the spongy grooves his squeezing had given it, like the grip on an arcade game handle, the grip of a pistol.

As the buyer passed with his father through the hallway on the way to the office, and before Philip could see them, he heard the two men stopping by the gun case. What was his father doing, Philip wondered, looking at a whole trove of displayed and pampered weapons? It would have been the least he could do to bring him in through the garage.

"You like Savages!" the buyer said.

"Yes," said his father.

"Good gun!" said the buyer. "Not jamming like the Thai gun, the Chinese made."

"Good guns, good guns," his father said. "Especially the shotguns. Little recoil." After a silence his father said "No kick."

"No kick! I like," the man said. "Better for you here," he said, his hand patting the fabric of his shoulder.

"Let's bring you down…" His father's voice trailed off in a cough as they descended the stairs.

Philip could see them now. His father sat behind his desk while the man pulled up his trouser legs, settling into the guest chair.

"Mr…?"

"Bo-ween," said the buyer.

"Mr. Boween, I want to show you a few things I've…" His father looked around him, at the plaques and awards, the certificates on the walls.

"I want to show you what I've been able to do. To get myself started on something new."

Boween coughed.

"But I'd like to tell you first that, well, you could sell that horse, you know. Sell it at a profit."

"'Scuse me?" Philip could see Boween's face clearer than his father's. The man was confused.

"I mean, you can re-sell it to someone else, for their kids, to have a horse. That's how good a price I'm giving you."

Boween dropped his head and looked straight at Philip's father.

"Six hundred."

"Six hundred. But you could re-sell it at a thousand, easy. I just can't go down cross river to do it now."

"But my children, they like the horse. We have a room," he said, twirling his finger in the air. "The room," he said. "Enough."

Philip's father leaned forward the way he always saw him do when making a deal, or trying to extract somebody's word on something.

"Don't tell it to one of your people, though, if you do sell."

"No. I will not," said Boween. "I could not explain presently. The reason. But no sale to my neighbors."

"Good," said his father. He leaned back and looked around himself again.

"That guy runnin' the country your people are living in? He's horrible."

Boween nodded.

"A nut."

"The man is a nut," his father repeated.

"Not even a good nut," said Boween. "He just a try-to-be nut."

Philip's father pointed. "There's a lot of building going on down where you are. You ever do any carpentry?"

"Carpen?" asked Boween.

"There are things. There are programs."

"Pogroms," Boween said flatly.

"Programs," his father said, a little loudly. "There must be someone in your group there. Well, I know there is. People who could get you on track."

Boween drummed his fingers.

"Computers!" his father said, looking each way with excitement and then straight back at him. "That's everything now. Computers are the world."

"Bill Gates the world. We just live in," Boween said, slapping his checkered, pulled-up pants. He gave a short, sharp laugh, as if someone were striking him.

Philip saw his father rocking slowly, truly or not-so-truly trying to hold back all-out laughter. Philip had seen it many times on deals.

"The Closer Laugh," his father called it. You recognized the teller and acknowledged the quality of the joke. But you did not lose yourself. You kept control.

"We build," said Boween, "the lost drives. We bring them back."

"You rebuild hard drives?"

"We image them. They see the image. They build themselves little pieces, by little pieces, until they are whole."

"I'll be damned," his father said. "I cannot, I repeat I cannot turn one of those sons of bitches on." He shook his head.

"New world," said Boween. "I can teach you turn on."

Philip's father was still looking at Boween, sizing him up, Philip knew. They were in different occupations, different areas, his father would say.

His father put his hands on his knees.

"You won't sell the horse there on your street."

"I will not."

"Promise."

"Promise, to cross my heart."

Then they looked at each other through the silence of the hot, thick air. Philip heard Rory's tail flicking, shooing flies from his hide.

"You know," his father said. "My people sucked mud."

Boween raised his eyebrows, brought his hand up to his mouth.

"The Turks. Made them march. Marched and marched them, till they died."

Boween nodded. "I have heard."

"So we started here too," his father went on. He coughed again. "We came with nothing."

His father pointed to a portrait of children standing before a building's steps with a kneeling man.

"All dead." His father swept the entire picture with his hand. "My grandparents' school class."

Boween ran his hands back and forth on his calves, and said "Tragedy."

"Who killed them? You want to know who killed them?"

His father pointed to the half-kneeling man, whose head bore a small round cap.

"Their teacher. Him."

Boween's eyes were wide now as he exhaled.

"He was a Turk. Once the fighting started, he marched them. He marched them and then he killed them."

Boween turned his hand back and forth slowly, looking at it as his father sat back down.

His father sat and stared at Boween. It seemed like forever to Philip. Boween smiled and frowned in an erratic way, shifting from one side of the chair to the next with an artificial energy, as if posing for pictures.

"I guess what I am trying to say here, Boween..."

Boween waited.

"Your hard drive business sounds great. Can't go wrong with it."

Boween nodded, reaching around, patting for his checkbook.

Philip's father came up out of his seat and then sat down. He had never taken his eye off Boween.

"Trust is what we have here, my people," said his father. "We trust here, in America. We learned we could do that."

"Truss," said Boween.

"What happened with the school? All that? Not here. That's for the other place."

His father pointed away, past the pictures. "That's for the other world."

Boween blinked, nodded.

Philip could tell his father was through when be broke the stare. But he still looked at the man when he brought the receipt ledger up out of his desk drawer. He took the check from Boween and put it under the thick glass paperweight. The sound of the writing pen could be heard in the silence, and the rip of the receipt from its perforated stub.

Philip rearranged himself on the floor. He still did not like the look on Boween's face. He satisfied himself that it wasn't anything about them, these people, which would be prejudiced. But still. There was a dark sparkle, an eagerness in his eyes.

The two men went up the stairs to get the boys.

The four of them walked out the door and up to the high point of the driveway in front of the dinner bell. The fathers stood talking and the younger boy got in the back jump seat of the long cab. The older brother put down the gate and pulled out the ramp as the barn hand walked Rory out. Rory put his head down, stamping a little, just before he walked up. The brother settled him in and put a blanket around him and gave him an apple.

Just before the brother got into the cab, Philip saw him lift a shoe tree out of the truck bed to make more room, and three or four horseshoes. The boy also lifted out a can of water and a long leather and sheepskin case, putting them up in the cab beside his little brother.

A swath of fire rankled down Philip's chest. He sat up abruptly. Another long, sick wave went down through his lungs as he watched his father and Boween shaking hands.

He reached for the swing blade. He knew how he would do it, like he'd seen it done in some action films. He wouldn't ask Boween and the boys for the gun at all. He would just walk quickly to one of the trailer's rear tires, making a tap punch along the siding. Then he could wedge the blade in and lean on it, pushing all of his weight until the tire blew out. Once the tire was flat, there would be nothing to talk about. He would be done.

Philip stood up in front of the door. He could not open it. He tightened his grip on the blade. He watched the men shaking hands, Boween walking around and getting behind the wheel, the two boys waving. He could not open the door.

Philip sat back on the bed. He raised the blade as far back behind his head as he could, bringing it down into the floor. It made a long crack in one of the ash planks that he knew his father would see. And Philip would see it forever as the clear and constant proof of his cowardice.

At the dinner table, two hours later, his father could see the tears in Philip's eyes.

"He's different," his father said.

"You don't know that," Philip said, refusing to meet his father's glance. The burning had subsided after he came downstairs, but he was still furious. He looked at the salt and pepper shakers. He thought of what he could do now. Refuse to work the horses. Open the pens and let them go.

"I think I made an impression on the man," his father said.

He would open the corral and all of the doors of the barn and let them out. He would shoo them away with the big sombrero the one hand, Fero, had brought him from Mexico.

Philip pushed his plate away. "I'd like to be excused."

"That's fine," the man said. "We got a feed stop tomorrow. Just a little to do."

Philip stood in front of him. The burning was coming back to him, back around his eyes, the bottom of his hair. He would have a few hours to read before it got dark. He would not come back down to sit with his father in front of the fire. He knew his father would not ask him to.

When he got to his room the clouds were bunching along the mountain ridge, the heather purple on their slopes, the road white. Cars were coming. Both the cars turned onto side roads and started climbing the hills. The third was a pick-up with a trailer, and Philip heard his father's cell phone ring.

Philip saw the truck with the trailer and Rory in it starting up their drive. The screen door slammed and his father walked out and waited in the yard. When Boween got out of the truck he motioned for the boys to stay inside and walked with Philip's father back into the house. They were standing in the kitchen where Philip couldn't see them.

"Problem?" Philip's father asked.

Boween was silent.

"You were selling to a neighbor? It was going to a family, wasn't it?"

Boween let out a breath and said, "No."

"I have called the bank," Boween said, "as I suspected. As I suspected, there is no sufficient money for the funds. Not now."

"Well," his father said.

"Maybe next month. I was wrong to come."

"No problem. No problem at all, Boween. I'll hold the…"

"Next month much problem too. Bills from doctors."

His father sighed.

"New lease for pasture," Boween went on. Philip heard Boween reach in his pocket and pull out the check. He heard a rip, then a sudden lurch to his father's voice, trying to stop him.

"Come with," said Boween.

Outside, Boween motioned to the older boy, who seemed to have the long leather case ready to hand out the passenger side. Boween took it and unzipped the back and pulled the long brown gun out of the sheepskin.

His father turned it around, looking at the finish on the wood. He lifted it up into an aim and sighted across the field. His father nestled the stock on the ridge of his waist, thinking.

"A Savage," said Boween.

The older brother turned around in the cab and sat hunched over. He ran his hands through his hair and shook his head. The men went around to the driver's door and shook hands. His father set the gun across his shoulders and rested each of his arms on it. Before the engine started, Philip thought he heard Boween say something to his father in another language.

Philip leaned back on his bed. At first he didn't think anything at all, but then he started thinking about the next day. He could not hug his father or really even thank him too strongly, as Philip was just becoming fourteen. And they were men. His mother would be back soon with 'Irin, and there would be time for such things.

Philip was tired. He shut his eyes. Before he passed into sleep, or even before he got to the filmy place he traveled through to get to where the true, black slumber would pull him down, he looked at the four walls around him. Around those walls were the walls of the hall, and around those the four sides of the house, and around those the square lines of their lot containing the house and the yard. And around their lot were the fields and around those the sharp squares of townships, and outside of them the long surveyors lines that marked away the counties, patches and patches of them lined up along the valley like foundation stones the rest of the state rose up from.

Down in the corner of one of the squares, as if he were looking from an airplane, he saw the truck with the trailer beginning to pass over the bridge into Parkersburg. The three men were not speaking to one another in the cab and Rory was back in the trailer, chewing, blanket-covered, unmindful of men or their danger, looking out through the high, silver girders arching up over the river in the sunlight.

Blue Moon Of Kentucky

Each night when I cannot sleep, when ribbons of words and calculations unravel in my head and the faces of those I love, present and past, appear in the darkness, accusing me of neglect, ignorance, apathy, lust—each of the allegations correct, and there's no hope of rest, I think of Kathleen Pearl, my seventh grade teacher. She is sitting on the steel desk she's started to occupy the day we met her, her legs crossed and her cat glasses perked high on the bridge of her nose. She had bright orange hair, piles of it that my mother puzzlingly called 'red,' and in the wet dark of her eyes were two white pinpoints that sparkled like high, cold Appalachian stars.

"We're going to be reading about a donkey," she said, smiling, as if that were enough to bring laughter that didn't come. "His name," she said, her legs flashing as they crossed in the other direction, "is Mr. Bones."

This got a few titters, like when Janet Cramer later said she would sing for us and that her father said she sang like a cow, and someone said he was right.

Mrs. Pearl was from Kentucky. She'd gone to a teacher's college in Paducah, but she was from the heart of the heart of that mystical place, from Harlan County, where mines stretched through the crooked ground like the legs of still-standing spiders. Her father had been a miner and was among the famous strikers, but he retired healthy, his lungs clear, taking up golf on a public course in the last years of his life. Pearl had five sons and an alcoholic husband who was a maintenance man up the hill at the high school. David was my age and the rest of the four treated me wonderfully, taking me to the swimming hole on their farm and pushing me out, on the rope's highest knot, over the stone-bottomed, honey colored water.

Kathleen let her accent flow freest when she talked about Mr. Bones, or any other book. Out in the town, at the bank or the P.O., she flattened the slant of the words, not wanting to be labelled a hillbilly. But when she talked about characters, myths, the shadowy, back-reaching chain of her strange ancestral people, her drawl reeled out like a poor whill's call.

Something wonderful flowed between her and us, especially we boys. The piles of red hair, the smile, the way she winked and bubbled and flowed. It seemed like some kind of strange visitation upon us. Visitation, the dour-mouthed Bible study teacher had called the descent of the Lord to Mary. With her and her felt stick-on Bible figures, everything was shame, a kind of veil of it, like the early evening's light there in the Great Lakes. The Kentuckian was her opposite—sitting on her desk! Kathleen was like the sun, rising, brightening the frost-flecked winter windows. All those years of remembering have brought me no distance from the first tremulous encounters with her—the drawl, the happy flash of limbs.

Sowash, my best friend, loved her too. We were each patrol leaders in our Scout troop, which met in the dark forest cabin of Red Culp's farm. On camping trips, we assembled between our bunks, in a crescent, the soft pornography we'd somehow obtained, looking down on its lurid arc as crumbs of our sandwiches dropped onto pictures of topless Chinese girls on hay bales. Sowash had a book called *Diary Of A Bad Girl* he'd found at his father's print shop. Its heroine had breasts so large they kept her off the swim team, and she let venomous creatures—Mrs. Shook would say Eden's very serpent—crawl in between her legs in a way we didn't quite yet understand.

Mr. Bones held little of our interest as all this went on. He was a donkey that a Tennessee farmer couldn't get to move the plow. It seemed quaint and stupid, even to her we suspected, as her Masefield line let the seafoam spray around us and Emily Dickinson talked about the sounds in her ears after she lay dead, stretched out on a silver infirmary table.

We were working up the basketball hierarchy at the Junior high, with me slightly better than Sowash but so many others, including my cousin David, putting both of us onto the benches.

"You like it, don't you?" she asked. Her college team, the Wildcats, were beating the Ohio State and Indiana teams into mush. "It's like life. It's better than life!" she said. "Everything is so speeded up, you don't know what's going to happen from one second to the next."

"The unknown," a girl at the back of the class said.

"You're darn tootin' it's the unknown," she said. "When something goes wrong in real life you go, back to the game, you say 'the ball can take funny bounces.'" A bird tapped the window with its needled beak.

"And everybody's outfits, the cheerleaders," looking over at Sowash, me, the boys in the second row. "The big, baggy pants on the boys. Everybody looks like they've been wrapped in a flag."

She pointed to Sowash. "Jon, have you been to a high school game?" He shook his head.

"Well boy howdy that's kind of"—she clucked her tongue, the red lipstick and her freckles, soft pecks of cloud—and looked out the window at the birdhouse. "That's kind of like not getting born yet."

"You need to go," she said. She pounded the lectern like she was beating out a scansion of Frost.

"The thing I'm saying is, nobody has much clothes on." She told us not to tell Swingle, the principal, that. Then she howled. "And the durn thing is, a lot of them look better like that." She winked down at Ron Drier, who turned purple as a turnip. The leaves were scorched and flattening outside the window. It was October, oddly summery, warm but with a crystal chill on everything, an extra sharpness laying in whatever was still green.

"I think you boys," she said, just before the bell, "will find a lot to like there. You like adventures. Just going is an adventure." She spun the other way on her desk.

"One bit of warning I have for y'all. Some of the..."

She held her tongue for a minute, letting us wonder what she was thinking. "Some of the big men here in town, the city fathers, as they get called in books." I looked over at Sowash. His father was one of them, but wasn't a sports man.

"They act like kids is what they do. They scream and call boys from the other team names."

She walked over to the window and pulled the blind shut. Bright bars of light floated over her face.

"Just remember what I said. They act like animals."

She was in silhouette now. Her body filled the air like a gift.

"Sit with the pep club," she said to me, then looked at Jon. "And remember, that Woody Guthrie song, 'There's More Pretty Girls Than One.'"

*　　　*　　　*

We were driving to the gym. High wheat and alfalfa stalks blew back and forth in the starlight. This part of the road was unpaved, and cinders pinged Legacy's Chevy and its dust curled silver under the moon before rolling over our windshield. Sowash drew on a Lucky. I looked back at him. When we hit a hole a mask of smoke floated away from his face.

The gym was enormous, square, the brute, jagged music of shouts pouring out of its walls like a beast awakening, growling itself out of slumber. Its corners didn't really seem sealed, so shafts of light poured down from them into the parking lot and grassland that would soon become concrete and fences.

Walking in, we had never seen a place so big. It was a home game. Our team, the Minutemen, were in blazing white silk with purple numerals. The Crestview team, populated with Appalachians and black kids from North Columbus, had dark gray jerseys flecked with red, and their wolf mascot, redder still, had a hungry tongue hanging out of its teeth.

The great orange ball spun from hand to hand in the air, its black stripes turning invisible in the loud, glad shouts and thumping feet, the squeak of sneakers echoing up to the rafters. The city men, especially Junior Schaeffer, the fat dentist, were just as Kathleen had said, yelling constantly at the referees and calling a black Crestview player a "pig nigger." They were taller than us, the players, and on jump balls our giant center, Claypool, pushed it out with a great claw-like pitch to his waiting forwards.

I followed Sowash, who seemed to know where he was going, into the dark cave of the bleachers. When we got to a space where light came down through the planking we looked up at the purple fifty and the white fifty of the pep club, a bright bank of pleated skirts that shook when they stood and clapped, then rustled when there was a foul and a free throw and they sat back down.

Their perfume and sweat mixed with the wood smell of the long oak planks, the sweet scent falling around us in an invisible cloud. We, too, felt invisible where we stood, belonging to shadows, scaffolds, a dusky blanket of the unseen. For some of the songs they twirled, their skirts turning and snapping, our eyes stunned by these flashes of treasure. I imagined their crotches throbbing like a bird's breast, a pattering tiny heart at the center of upturned wings. At halftime the light around us became unsplintered, even, like the blue light in a refrigerator.

Maybe I only imagined the scent between their legs getting stronger, like a mist of the Lake Effect, like wood smoke. I wanted to press my hands on the turning shapes, the white, immaculate fabric covering the most girl parts of them. One of the purple crew looked underneath and gave us a scolding smile, knowing we saw this as life, life, or at least the heart of life, where there was no thing of beauty that was not forbidden.

My soul blazed with what I was seeing, with the deep alteration it had made.

The front of my pants contained a long, mindless and hungry stone.

Someone yelled at us from behind. It was Detlef Yoder, the Yugoslav janitor whose name we knew from the giant elastic band bearing it, his boxer shorts riding up above his unstrapped overalls. Sowash explained he'd dropped his wallet—"billfold" we called them—under the bleachers, and Yoder squinched up his face, skeptical. All boys lie. All horny boys lie absolutely.

An exit door was open ahead of us, filled with the field's alfalfa. The Minutemen were winning. We too had won something enormous. It was the golden time we wished for, the argot we were meant to see, to touch. Out in the cold October air we ran till our bodies glowed.

* * *

Kathleen watched us closely in the following days, as if she was waiting for us to tell her something. She walked into class, her notebooks nestled against her breasts, smiling only at Jon and me. She had changed. We had been welcomed into a new place by her knowingness. When she set down her books, or at the end of class when she gathered them up, she had a terrible, bothersome smile.

When Jon and I walked in the hall alone she finally asked us. "What'd you think of the game?"

"Great," we said.

"Had to have been some high shots the way your necks are craned back. Looks like you're looking at the ceiling," she said, laughing. "Detlef mows my yard, dear boys."

Sowash and I looked at each other.

"Those Serbs don't keep any secrets," she said, wagging her finger. Then she shrieked — the full Appalachian squeal.

I didn't know about Sowash, but I felt wonderfully discovered somehow, taller, airier and more mobile. In that instant, and for some time afterward, all my dread disappeared, my fear falling behind my mind's new growth, new knowledge, new stubble that was growing with arrogance from my smooth nicked chin. I was a tree, brimmed with some strange new sap of ardor, a changeling, and when I signaled to Sowash to come with me, to run from her laughter, I felt swept clean by the sun, like the lawn we raced to and whose shadows slid and whirled around our feet.

Flashbox

Werner couldn't bring Cheney to look at him for more than a few seconds at a time. Cheney and his funeral homes had been clients for years, but the recent corporate takeovers, the Swedish holding company conglomerations, had made Cheney a jittery, almost spastic man to take a meeting with. Before, when he and his brothers were on their own, Cheney could discuss cases with the same somber assurance with which he floated through a room at calling hours, or fairly and thoroughly took a crumbling family through the options of the casket room.

Now the man's margins were squeezing him, he said, almost to ...well...the obvious term would cause him to smirk in his flinty way that unsheathed his black-edged incisors, something both men preferred he never, ever do.

Cheney's acquisition people were going for after-market caskets to save change. One might wonder what, on Earth, an after-market casket might be, but it is really just one with a significant defect, a frame boarding of cheaper wood than usual, handles attached with screws rather than brass or tempered steel. It was like the new Volvos Werner was seeing in the mid-oughts: so much more plastic, not even the pretense of synthetic wood.

But the lifts and vertical crypts were what was worrying Werner and the liability insurers much more. As the outskirts of Columbus—particularly its eastern suburbs—were growing more congested, space in the cemeteries was at a premium. When Werner's daughter's boyfriend died of a heroin overdose out in L.A., the boy's plot—which his Zurich banker father could afford—was over six figures. Since it was next to Marilyn Monroe's and Merv Griffin's, it was like buying a house next to theirs. Access to eternity was no different than an immured, breeze-blessed view of ocean frontage. It was all location, location, location.

Vertical crypts had been a Jewish phenomenon for decades. Some outfit out of Chicago had started the practice for Gold Coast machers, and Werner remembered that one of Saul Bellow's shysters in *Humboldt's Gift* had sold crypts where the rabbinically dispensed bodies could not lie flat, but had to spend the sojourn to Judgment Day hunched up like in the bad middle seat on a small airplane.

Patents on vertical crypts were snatched up initially by Forest Lawn, and the first of them, used by Cheney's firms, stood like enormous beige refrigerators on the freeway hilltops leading down into Norwalk and grittier points east.

It took a hydraulic lift to elevate a casket into one of these things. Interior elevators were massive, expensive, and putting grandpa's bier onto a secure platform and hoisting it up four or five stories had proved pretty foolproof. The crane operators were pros, expensive pros, and if a coffin shifted a bit it could be maneuvered with remote levers to nose its way into the latest, freshest smelling drawer of the mausoleum.

Werner spent a lot of time appeasing the underwriters, appeasing claims people, but most of all cajoling, pushing, hammering on Cheney to cut where the cutting made sense. Hydra-lifts were in the set of nonsense members, as Jack would have said in his symbolic logic days. The lifts didn't even get easy coverage for their usual uses: car jacks, penile implants. Lifting coffins struck Jack as beyond the pale, but consultants had put the issue to rest—data heads with spreadsheets had a way of impressing nonquantitative risk analysts.

And there were larger liabilities, by far, than the lift hydraulics. Scores of cases arose from mixing remains, pooling groups of different ashes and bone. Werner cursed these few new sizable blocks of cases—massive clusters of them, continents really—being handed to him in the dissipating days of his partnership as a litigation "generalist." The mixture cases were really just errors of shelving and organization and logging—two peoples' ashes could go in the same urn. One woman's ashes could be spread into three containers. Bone fragments could be taken out of ash clusters and put into trays, unlabeled and then finally lost.

These tracing mistakes could yield big verdicts for the plaintiffs' bar, especially if you had panels of people themselves approaching death. For all the living relatives' talk of the importance of their departed's souls, their spirits, how nothing and no one belonged to us except in memory, Werner marveled at how easily their tattered grief could be stoked into outrage by the right plaintiff's lawyer fanning his fingers through the right crisp piles of imagined cash.

Remains errors had started, at least for Werner, in his first job at a big firm, about twenty-five years before. A DC-10 had crashed into some airport buildings in a large Latin American capital. It was an American airline, and the pilot, confused by ground fog, had mistaken an active taxiway with the standard landing apron handed off to "heavy" wide bodies like the one he was flying—those of two hundred thousand tons or more. All 141 people on the plane were killed, along with fifteen in the tiny buildings the landing gear had grabbed and lifted like a rodent in an eagle's talons.

He had lived in a Sheraton in the middle of the city and was working out settlements with the families. It was the first he had ever learned of econometric forecasting and actuarial ratios. Damages to the victims' survivors could involve calculations based on where their relatives had been sitting; how much more pain and suffering—shock, really—someone with a clear view out a window had to endure as opposed to a person in a rear seat, in the center, with no idea of what was happening even in the instant of their death.

Identifying the remains had been daunting. The only accurate word for it was barely controlled taxonomies. His crew of associates had to work with marginally competent forensic pathologists and coroners. At first fingerprints and dental records yielded accurate matchings: 110 conclusives, and approximately fifty probable IDs or "probs," as they were called—identification with forty-five to sixty percent likely accuracy.

This was enough (it had to be) to satisfy almost every one of the families. These were pious, lower-middle-class Catholics from the peripheral suburbs, and it was important to have a body to bury, some physical thing to eulogize and commemorate, to put into the ground and provide a memorial for future visitations. The press coverage had been lurid, and the restoration of dignity to these peoples' loss had become—among Werner's colleagues—a preoccupation, if not an obsession.

It was then that they found the extra body, three days after the last funeral.

A completely unrecognizable torso had been wedged between the main ground building and a smaller, adjacent shed that housed turbines and compression machinery. Since the plane had fragmented on impact, it was no more likely the body had been a ground victim than a passenger. It threw all fifty probable IDs into disarray. Every family had gotten a body or a part of a body — there were no empty-handed heirs—but clearly now a number of the dead had divided into a multiple person, a person and somebody else, as it were, and there was no way of telling who the body belonged to without unravelling everything. The forty-five to sixty percent uncertainty had divided by…how much? By one, in a sense. But one multiplied by that fifty, and coming at the worst possible time.

In the end the lawyers had left things exactly as they were. The capital police and national safety institute, dozens of men breathing mescal fumes, took the firm's advice to bury the body in an unmarked utility grave in one of the unmarked provincial military cemeteries.

Werner was slain by how the rights and wrongs of a single action like this could burn forward and backward through time, like the rays of Borges's all-encompassing Zohar, leaving the decision-maker immobilized. But that frozen volition had to be transformed into something resembling true decisiveness. Werner woke at night often with thoughts of the single and singular body, free to be thought of as known or unknown. He remembered the scene in *Lawrence of Arabia* where Allenby could not resign himself to a troop commitment that he knows is essential but will cost him many men. "Do nothing," Lawrence tells him. "It is often best."

"Yeah," Cheney said when this was recounted to him. "That's a goddam shame. But this ain't Mexico, and the loved one's lawyers have my balls dropping like the Dow on a humid day. They noticed the deposition of my guy who was putting the transition boxes together in his own garage. He labelled. He fiddled and faddled. But you know what he did too?"

Werner ran the nail of his finger along the ridge of a file.

"He put some of the ash segments in single piles. Not enough boxes."

Werner knew there were few defenses to such an action. Though the relatives didn't find out till much later, they were devastated. Plaintiffs' class action lawyers were crawling like roaches across the floor when the light was switched on. Class certifications were pouring into the courts, districted through every jurisdiction where Cheney had homes and a long history of tomb and graveyard leases.

A new device was available to undercut the intermixture cases. He'd seen one at a trade show. Its ends looked exactly like the blank face of the wide-screen, wall-mounted TV in the break room at Cheney's Mt. Vernon home, where he sat with a ream of slip-and-fall files generated by the old man's refusal to sprinkle winter parking lots with something cinder-like. Walking to the Fleetwood limousine, taking grandma on her last ride down, falling on your ass. This was not dignified.

The crematoria box at the trade show mimicked this pre-game delivery device, signaling that the box contained something of ingenious uniqueness and internal capabilities—"applications" as they were now called—never seen before by the feckless, non-digital eye. They called it the Flashbox.

Werner let out a sigh of satisfaction, knowing Cheney would go—for the right price—for all cremations to go to the joint in the Flashbox. Bodies had always been wrapped in shrouds and placed four to six in the twelve-by-twenty-foot blast furnace whose whale-backed roof stuck up out of the crematorium on a grimy Mt. Vernon hillside. Loose bodies and too much space is what led to the ash mixtures, the scattering of burning tissue, the interspersal of bone fragments and black, obsidian-glittered outlines of shins and eye sockets.

But the Flashbox put four bodies at a time into quadrants of heavy-gauge separators around a much lighter-gauge shell. In the ten minutes of burning, and even if the outer shell incinerated, every body stayed contained in its own shaft, its own last pathetic verst of real estate. It made Werner think of the grave-size answer to Tolstoy's story "How Much Land Does a Man Need?" The quadrants maintained, the ashes never mixed in the air, even during the fiercest height of the burning. Each corpse minded its own business and exited largely as it had gone in.

Where had he gone wrong in this second foray with Alicia, in hindsight a walk down the aisle of hell? He had not compartmentalized. He brought the irritations of litigation home to the simplest marital disagreements. He approached his daughter's questions with something akin to a deposition checklist, pounding the problems down like whack-a-moles, never clouding his resolutions with emotion, with the necessity of adequate, even of blundering, feeling.

He could not say lawyering had ruined his life, stuffing its methodologies into familial contention. But the question was whether he was that way already. The question was whether the profession furnished him with tools of evasion, coldness, an efficiency that didn't have the time to work through the dim, warm tunnels of love.

He closed in on family happiness, as well as family strife, with all the fury and order of the Flashbox. Everyone leaned into him, seeking solace, seeking a common ground of problem-solving. But he kept them separate, the dust and shards and ashes of three hearts never permitted to float, as they naturally might, into a single cloud. Black and white. If genius wore white, then life wore white. What wore black was life and white's opposite. And it throbbed in front of Jack's face now, like the blotches that came up when he closed his eyes.

When Werner got up he passed the bathroom where Cheney was combing his hair with the door open. He was hunched over, a corpse himself, an osteoparitic lump growing like some hideous vegetable from under his threadbare, tickweave jacket. Werner winced at how the man licked his comb before running it through the black, greasy flops that hung down from his orange pate.

Cheney himself was on his third marriage. Women liked "undertaker fellas," as Cheney called them—they did well, they kept their work to themselves, the showing home doubled as their own large mansion. There was no obsolescence. People kept dying. Every inch of those six dug feet had gold in it.

And Cheney's weirdness, his darkness, his mordancy, he had turned it into affability, a presentation that could pass for true sympathy. He had just taken a painful weakness—his alienness—and by doubling down on it had polished it into a marketing powerhouse.

*　　　*　　　*

The first lift burial would be later that day. The new burial, that is, with the first refitted lift. The prongs were supposedly like the talons holding a rocket's fuselage. The price had pleased Cheney, and the beneficiary of it all, a retired Air Force lieutenant colonel, would enjoy the entire military sendoff. Riflemen with white gloves, twenty-one-gun salute, the flag folded and whisperingly given to the widow.

Werner stopped back at his office to finish a couple of motions, and when he got into the Volvo, the starter skipped, all the dash lights lit up, and the check-engine light sputtered and then faded peaceably away. There were all kinds of little things like this that needed fixed. When he drove by the house on the way to Bucyrus Cemetery, there she was—Gloria—watering her flowerbed with a malfunctioning hose. The spray came back onto the front of her blouse. He honked and waved, and she shrugged, smiling. She spread her arms so he could see the dark buds of her nipples. There were many things about her he would miss.

The cemetery was crowded. The men Durbin had recommended were fully uniformed, standing at parade rest, which allowed them to take handkerchiefs out of their pockets and dab their faces from the heat.

There was a white ring of chrysanthemums around the flagged coffin. He had been too young to be in the Big One, but was some kind of child prisoner in a Japanese camp with his mother, his father receiving a harsher fate which nonetheless kept his son inspired, enthused, a drinker of the Kool-Aid of the crossed rifles.

Werner sat in the back, among the minority of the nonmilitary. Across the crowd of white officers caps he saw the bowed heads of the widow and adult children. The first speaker, a full colonel, moaned of a quickly degenerating culture. The second, also a colonel, spoke of the deceased's decency with prisoners after the fall of the Hue citadel. He had been a captain and, for whatever it meant, the Tet Offensive had made him a "humbler" but "more warlike" soldier.

When the speeches were over the riflemen let off their reports, and the bugler got his taps right, extending the last note with a somber, unnecessary emphasis. The flag was folded, the triangle handed over with the whispered presentation, and the widow nodded, like an animal hearing something in the ground.

The coffin was lifted onto the platform, and Werner admired the burnished mahogany. No wonder the joints got thousands for them. No wonder Jessica Mitford and the funeral muckrakers went after the Cheneys of the world with hot tongs. Still, the sun gleamed on the burnished wood like a polished floor, and the reflection of the elms poured over its length in patches of green and crumbling bark. Werner noticed one of the struts was colored differently than the others.

Bagpipes played. So many of Werner's older colleagues would say "Just bagpipes. Bagpipes are what I want." The droning notes covered the sound of the lift, which moved like a great water bird, pecking its beak up toward the wall of sparkling granite. The platform moved forward, nosing toward the open square which would keep the man, as the chaplain had said, like a sleeping child until the dead (similarly situated) were called up by the Redeemer.

There was what appeared to be an extra rifle shot, a mistaken discharge that caused the bagpipes to halt and, in the sun-thick silence, the slightest of collective gasps passing over the crowd and up into the echoing blue.

But it was a strut, the discolored one, snapping like a burning twig and letting the coffin slide out like a tilted missile and head toward the hollow center of the crowd. People screamed and took two, three steps backward as the blur of it fell with gravity's awful certainty, the certainty of crashing planes and the hanged man's body killing itself by the mere act of dropping.

It sounded like thunder hitting the ground, the planks in turn snapping again, flying apart like paper as the satin interior let the body explode like a water balloon, splashing every front seat with embalming fluid, formaldehyde, shards of new-softened flesh and purplish bags of guts squirting out through the seams in the dead officer's dress whites.

People ran, screaming. Two women fainted. Someone was quick enough to call unnecessary paramedics so the sirens could be heard immediately, drowning out everything, red lights throbbing above the distant traffic.

Werner saw Cheney on his cellphone, calling in a crew. His own people wouldn't be enough for this. It would take OH-trans, regulatory bodies, goons in hazmat suits to meet all the state specifics and ordinances for an airborne toxic event. The widow and kids were hustled into the limos, Cheney motioning toward them with trembling, hesitant hands. The hands that comforted grief, that smoothed sobbing shoulders, that ran the comb through the greasy, Mongol tent flaps of his hair.

Werner's car wouldn't start at first. How do you ask for jumper cables at a funeral? Do you bring in one of the little battery trucks from AAA?

When it finally came to life Werner knew it would get fixed. Everything would get fixed in the end. What he saw around him was a crowded quarter of work, billable hours flowing out of a black, crepe-strung horn of plenty.

He drove slowly back to the office, the sirens fading under the sound of his defective, dieseling engine. The neighborhoods were normal, unaffected. The sun still shone with its utmost perfection.

But a breeze had come up. The small pile of mail that had been left on his office stoop was blowing out from its inky, broken rubber band. When he got out and started walking in, he saw the return address of a divorce firm he knew of on the upper corners of the fat envelopes. They were like the flags of some new, menacing country, making a blue-white trail up over the brick steps.

Rain In The Heart

The cinderblock had fallen from the bridge overpass, plunging through the windshield of the mother's car, bashing her head so badly her foot left the accelerator and she drifted over into the side lane near the Overland Avenue exit. It would begin to kill her slowly, but looked like it already had—her face a mound of scarlet mush that fell back against the headrest, which dripped with backsplatter, bone fragments, rivers of blood thickening on the elegant leather seat. None of her four kids were with her. No errand items. No dogs or purchases.

She wasn't an immediate DOA, so an ambulance took her up to Cedars, where Lil's friend Bev was a nurse in the ER. So much blood soaked through the sheets they kept putting new ones on her. The orderlies had a drill where they could whip the bloody one out as the new sheet floated downward, billowing, curved like a quiet parachute in the cave of sound—screams, shouts, metal clanging—that still surrounded all of the beds. It was the plague time. People stayed away from hospitals. But ERs were clamorous places—pleas and screams and pleas again from out of the mounds of blankets and gauze.

Her husband was traveling and the kids were taken to an aunt's. Lil went over for a while. Their faces were so white and unbelieving that they could not cry. Sometimes they stood in a row and sometimes the row of them placed itself on the couch as the aunt and a cousin brought them glasses of water. Lil wondered who had told them without the father there. There were people at hospitals, social workers, that had such jobs. Death-messengers, like oncologists.

Lil wanted to ask Bev how such messages were delivered. But Bev was beside herself in the café now where they talked. She had just come from the house and had been in the ER when the interns were pumping the mother's chest.

Bev had seen a lot—small plane crashes, commuter train suicides with heads and hands cut off by rails, explosions at chemical labs where the stuff couldn't be put out and burned whole hands and arms down to the bone. But Bev had never seen anything this bad, a head wound this severe. The mother had no facial skin intact, and a corner of the block had gouged out an eyeball and flattened her cranium, its centerless squares having left their exact footprint on her forehead and the beginnings of her scalp. They had shaved her head in case there was hope of getting her up into surgery.

But this was the worst, Bev said. She would talk for a minute and then start sobbing, looking down at the bowl of milk that some cereal—was the waitress sleeping?—was supposed to go in. She could hardly look at Lil. But when she did her eyes were so red and puffed that Lil imagined her as the swollen purple head of the woman herself. Bev, a nurse for thirty-five years, told Lil there was motion in the woman's hand as she held it, tremors that were probably involuntary final twitches, the organism trying to preserve itself, trying to stay a few more minutes in the world.

Bev put her head in her squared arms planted on the formica. Lil reached out and grabbed her arm, her head.

"There was nothing left of her face," Bev said, muffled, choking, looking up but out the window. It took a long time for her to meet Lil's eyes. Lil felt helpless, imagining the helplessness of all nurses. How do you keep your head on straight with an assembly line of gunshot wounds, glass shards pulsing from the flesh of car crash victims, severed hands bundled in towels beside bodies while nurses ran around looking for a refrigerator key, trying to save the chilly wrist for the reattachment surgeons.

"Honey, I couldn't stand it. I couldn't stand there and look, and I'm the nurse." "Fuck," she said. Lil tried to support one arm and saw what was left of the washed-off blood on Bev's skin, faded but with its edges sharp, like the sea-reaching splotches of land on a map.

When Lil asked the waiters for ice in a hand towel Bev waved her away, waved away the manager wondering what was wrong. Her lips trembled as the tears slid off of them, and when she looked at Lil it was like she was looking through a window, looking out a door that led to pastures, meadows of death.

Lil was twenty minutes late to her class. The teaching assistant looked at her warily, looked down at the nail marks Bev's fingers had left in the back of her hand.

"I'm not OK. Not OK. I can't be here today."

But she had to be. The other teachers and staff were strapped. They needed her. The assistant brought a paper by, knowing what had upset Lil. The headline called the mother's death another "infrastructure accident." There were many of them now. Under the banner was a "news analysis" editorial calling for taxes, grants, anything to fix the high, crumbling stone that was falling down everywhere.

Lil pushed the paper aside and looked out on her class of problem kids, an audience of what was now called the developmentally disabled. She saw their constant agitation as a kind of light around their bodies. Gravity was like a cloak, the lightest garment they could slip out of. A silk robe, a kimono. Alison was her cartwheeler, her hand-stander. She spun across the room on her stiff-limbed windmill, calloused hands, hair wagging. She taught Tom, and later Dmitri, to stand on their heads, first with supporting hands and then with nothing but their heads, the warm pillows of young hair cupping their skulls with soft certainty. Allison put her classmates into circles, first still and then moving, like ancient Maypole spinners or toddlers playing ring-around. Her twin, Amy, brought in sticks and branches which she bent adeptly into animals.

They, the lot of them, could be aggressive. The girls, oddly, much more than the boys. If a hand slipped, if a step in the dance was missed, a girl might slap another, push her so her neck jerked and her hair came out of its morning-Mother arrangement.

Dmitri was among the mollifiers, the calmers. The psychiatrist Jill consulted with told her about Melanie Klein, who had written of "flips" from violent to peaceful and back again, something children carried from their early agons with their mothers, first nurturing sources and then enemies to be eviscerated. Lil's kids riffed on this model, holding their companions' shoulders and minutes later karate-chopping the bottoms of their backs.

Dmitri was the peacemaker, infallibly calling for calm, pulling people apart. This sheriff's role came to him when he was most quiet and depressed. The same cloud that passed its mist over his face had a kind of pixie dust that stopped the clamor of his fellow spinners and dancers. He had a touch, and in the touch Lil imagined a gift, something almost supernatural, but pouring out of the grittiest earthiness and normalcy.

One girl, in an epileptic fit, threw books around the room like a spinning machine. Dmitri timed the spokes of her hands—lots of these kids, some high intelligent Aspergers with an intuitive physics—and made sure nobody became a target. One boy, two boys tried to drop a globe from the high bookshelf they stood on. They were waiting for the right enemy, a certain snide redheaded girl. Dmitri stood below their perch. If you want to hit something, hit me. Drop it and I'll catch it.

He not only caught it but snagged it on the tips of his fingers, like a basketball player. He bounced it on his palms and watching him, Lil thought of Charlie Chaplin in *The Great Dictator*, Hitler passing the globe around like a basketball.

The Glover sisters were in one of their imaginary cooking fits, funneling their neurosis into a kind of Formula One baking run-off. They couldn't have a lighter or be in the kitchen, so all they could do was pull down bowls from the cupboards, whip the butter, load it all up with flower and yeast. Once, in an earthquake, their concoction swayed like the tiny waves of a reservoir. They pushed the pastel china together with air-hockey velocity, but could tell—again from their disorder—to push just hard enough to avoid breaking the bowls. Once they miscalculated, and geysers of unwhipped gunk flew out and spread across the pleats of their dresses.

The boys liked the rough tones of this supposedly gentle gaggle of females. The expected manner of the cooking, too, had a clamor much louder than seemed possible. Doug Grosso loved this, leaning forward like a zoo creature behind its glass. Jim Roper, whose class picture revealed a fly on his head, egged them on—'Go girl. Go bitch' in a soft tone they couldn't hear.

Dmitri would laugh, in his gulping, asthmatic, but somehow patois-like streams of hilarity. He'd tapped out a rhythm on his knees, trying to follow the calf-slapping of Grosso. Lil saw Dmitri as the keel in this showboat, steadying, steadying it as the whole thing started slipping and collapsing. He was good, as was Grosso, with the girls, who were far more crazed than the boys, manic pools of estrogenic explosion. Lil locked up all the knives and scissors, but worried even about the bowl shards, even the girls' clean, fast-growing nails. She thought of the psych-techs, burly bouncer-types in the Cedars 5150 wards, who of course the school could not afford. The funding gaps were cloying at first, then infuriating. She bought texts out of her paycheck, brought food from home as the girls' weights were dropping. Boys took pieces of the food gratefully and walked around eating it, their skin shimmering with the white pallor of the hungry.

The acrobats—that's what she called them—lined up before their stunts—sweet or macabre—like a formless row of sagging shacks. Then each would start to break away, as if in something modernly choreographed. One girl—Lil was terrible with names, a deficit for a teacher—told Lil she felt like she was going to "buth open." What she would do is simply hold her breath and puff out her cheeks like a blowfish. Her whole body would inflate—her stomach and tiny breasts, and make a metal balloon inflating sound, that kind of tinny, unfolding crinkle. She told Lil she never thought of anything because she was afraid she'd become the thing she was thinking of. After learning a little Darwin in biology, and with Lil spotting bulimia symptoms, the girl would suddenly throw out crazed savant phrases, like "Everything looks for something softer than itself to eat."

One of the cartwheelers spun through, knocking a ruler and pencil sharpener off Lil's desk.

An older girl, who looked so much like the Darwin girl they could be twins, had body separation and skin-shift hallucinations, talking about how, at certain times of the day, her head had shifted a little to the left. Or her eyes, her skull, the thoughts coming forward out of it like a tiny circus megaphone. The articulation of this always changed, but it was always a shift, a tilt. Usually to the left.

Disembodiment was a constant mean for these kids. Less of them were the usual fare—like in other homes—of self-harmers, cutters, skin gougers, water-running scalders. They stood entirely to the side of themselves, so the harming would seem like they were harming somebody else. They felt their lives were being lived by somebody else. They loved the East European torture movies, but that was as far as true slashing and bludgeoning would go. For Lil, as ashamed as she would be to admit it, the lurid movies were bringers of peace, flickering buffers in the dark.

Dmitri never spoke of displacement, of distancing, or what the DSM called 'splintering.' He could be wildly eccentric, bugging out his eyes, pretzeling his arms. But he had, by Lil's lights, grown into himself, robustly embraced who he was with all of its warts and flashes of unravelling. He didn't seem to need the others, which Lil saw as a kind of strength. He was happy in his own company. Most of her kids were hard and incomplete, not having come into their characters, the fullness of their personalities. They were like kits, beginning to fill with the wind of themselves like the puffer girl. But Dmitri filled all of himself, catching hold of some early branch of maturity.

His eyes were smooth, as calm as a windless pond. Their blue, blue sameness made Lil want to believe in God.

When the pandemic came, the school stayed in session. It was in one of the red counties whose governments were skeptical of masking, bureaucrats, federal entities handing out "guidelines" that had so far seemed fruitless.

Her acrobats were there each day, spinning with masks on, standing upside down and pulling the bottom of the cloth off their chins so they could breathe and shout. They brought all of their old selves with them, but with a new sense of both fearfulness and joy. Following the lockdown's tiny steps filled them with wonder, made them part of adult life, made their lives belong to the world.

When Dmitri wasn't back by the fourth day she wondered if he'd shown symptoms and his mother had sequestered him. Surely it was something the woman was controlling, finding the limits of. He had not missed a class in three years.

She felt a hole quivering in the space of the room where he always sat. But he was so silent so much of the time that the empty space couldn't be silent too. The clatter and laughter of the new-masked spinners filled out the square of his clean emptiness, his chilly Buddha calm. A Buddha stillness. That was the thing about him. Lil felt she had finally happened on its truest description. She liked the odd assessment. She liked the idea of it.

When Lil called his mother's cell—everyone's mobiles were on an 8 X by X app—they went unanswered, even when she tried every three or four hours. Lil called Bev at her nurse's station and asked if she'd heard from anyone at the house or anyone who knew him. Bev's voice was cagey. She said that something was going on. She didn't want to talk about it, felt that she couldn't. Her clipped snippets took on an old-fashioned, gossipy tone as she hedged and deflected, the kind of guarded jabber she remembered from the days of party lines. This absence of information from an old confidant chilled and irritated her. Toward the end of the call, in a near-whisper that made Lil's stomach flip, Bev said Lil might want to turn on the TV.

After about an hour and a half Dmitri's school picture came up on the screen. Lil picked up the remote but it wouldn't work. She checked the batteries. The area of the school she sat in had such poor reception, its open spaces and athletic wings pocketing voices and then bursting them back. She finally got the sound on, but it was just as his face was fading, still staring out at her with the eyes that had made her breathless so short a time ago.

Dmitri was missing, was all she could conclude. She dialed the assistant principal, the school nurse and counselor, people she had true friendships with. He was missing. Missing. She went back through her thoughts of him, the long, filmlike row of images. She wondered how far he could get if he'd just left home. Five miles. Twenty-five miles. He had that kind of energy, that sureness of purpose.

* * *

It was Dmitri who had dislodged the piece of concrete from the overpass. Someone had seen him run from the missing square with a steel rod or a crowbar. Those were the allegations. He had been released on his own recognizance, to the mother who never picked up the phone.

Lil went to the wastebasket in the media room and vomited, the surge of it splashing and smearing the ink on the crumpled paper. When her stomach was empty and her head blank—at least for now—she went into her office, thanking God it was study hall so she could keep her door locked. The tears kept falling, in neat, streaming drops down onto her blotter. She pushed her keyboard toward the monitor to keep it dry.

She felt there was nothing left for her now, in her heart or what was left of her head. She took out her Xanax, pear-shaped light peach pills, and downed four of them with a bottle of Fiji water. "It will break you down." It's what her father had said about working with kids like this. "It breaks you down." It was worth it, she thought, the fracturing, the personal crumbling. She was a passenger on their train, setting each one of them down in a cracked plastic but still useable seat. She built on that, that moving forward. She walked now in her thoughts through the sun and shadow of the imagined, racing, voice-filled cars.

Bev would have known Lil had seen this all already. She scrolled through the Beverlys in her contacts, even though she knew her number by heart. They would get someone in to see him. Somebody other than a lawyer.

In a newspaper quiz the day before, she learned that Hitler was known to have loved and treated with special attention his loud pen of shepherds. For hours, it was the only thing she could think about. In the next couple of days, as details developed, she could not rid herself of the image—the small man leaning down in his perfectly pressed officer's uniform, taking pieces of meat out of a bowl and placing them, with the utmost gentleness, into each one of the upturned mouths.

Hard Times

Carothers saw something familiar in the gait, the carriage of the golfer lifting the iron out of his bag and walking toward the tee. The car would be stopped for a minute or two, and he'd soon be able to tell for sure. This was one of the few spots where you could see into Indian Hill, its curtain of ancient oaks hiding almost all of it from the peering eyes of non-members, the lowly and unblessed, the rest of the world. Carothers thought of the line he loved from a novel he couldn't remember much else of, how the settled stance of golfers looked to passers-by like the digging of their sharp cleats into the broad backs of the poor.

He could see—he could tell from the way the man tested his long swing—that indeed it was Lefferts, his broker, the head of the small firm that had always handled his and his late wife's investments. It was the way the player craned his head out at the Par-5, like a tortoise, the leathery stalk of his neck giving a wobbling periscope access to his eyes, which were shadeless and squinting and concentrated like a sniper at a distant target.

Lefferts swung, and Carothers recognized the hands, the way they let the club slide through them till the wood caught in his rested, satisfied grip. He always held documents that way, and sometimes gave them the same slow, scrutinizing, amphibious gaze.

Carothers drove on, remembering the early meetings with the broker in the heady, flush mid-eighties. Lefferts had the same aloof jauntiness, the same finger-brush of contempt when Carothers and his wife sat down and craned their heads over the portfolio spread across his Biedemeyer desk. Ski equipment stood in the corner of the office, and when Carothers looked at it, another emblem of the unaffordable on his high school principal's salary, he detected Lefferts' acknowledgment of this fact. And something else: a satisfaction, if not a smugness, at the lesser state of his client, a muted gloating in his one pale wandering eye.

The message in that look, transmitted to Mrs. Carothers' heirs, was that she had been handed less than her entitlement, and that this upper boundary of what she could obtain was a fated, possibly even a sought-after state. Carothers felt the awful fact of it easing out of his wife's quick hopefulness, her eager reaching at things that came with greater risk and greater reward. Lefferts would turn his palms up, slowly shake his satisfied head, and look—Carothers could testify to it—over toward the racing skis in the dull room's corner.

Carothers' yields on his investments stayed steady in the first years after Alice was gone. The bonds paid at a normal coupon rate for municipalities, steady, nothing exciting, and the equities rose and fell like mushrooms in the rich, warm quiet of the country's collective wealth—predictable but startling in their distentions, their known shapes richened and bursting with unknown energies, unseeable forces. Carothers was happy overall. The yields let him travel, guided him in his first timid steps into the gulf left by Alice's loss.

Even the dips were tolerable, cushioned by the broker's spread—the big one in '87, the little ones that sputtered in from year to year, usually in 3-year cycles. Lefferts called them adjustment farts, and they never came up except in cocktail conversation. It was never enough, or Carothers never thought it was enough, to warrant the broker's drawing it to his attention. Their bi-yearly meetings now took the form of lunches at San Domenico, an elegant eatery on the Ohio River waterfront near Reds Stadium that Carothers had noticed boarded up the week before. Things had to be bad for that place to go under. It was one of the indicators.

Carothers had usually let Alice look at the statements. For all his superior understanding of economics, he felt reassured that anything significant—not just something big—would jump up at her and cause her to come to him for an explanation. The joke between them was that the account number on their statements, a random merger of letters and the last four digits of his social security number, had in fact only the last four digits of that holiest, most secret of signifiers. The first group of letters was blocked by Xs, like on a credit card receipt. He found this puzzling, but never warranting an inquiry to Lefferts. In fact, after Alice, he'd left most of the statements unopened. They gathered space in a shoe box on a closet shelf.

The first dive statement—that's what they were called—arrived in the early Summer. He couldn't remember what had made him open it, but of course it had to have been the news. Financiers were buying newspapers and brokerages with debt commitments that Carothers had never heard of before, and didn't even think possible. He'd been at San Domenico, pressing the Wall Street Journal along the middle of each open page, so that it lay in vertical quarters along the side of his breakfast plate. He watched a tugboat plow the white-brown wavelets of the river as he read; it looked like it was melting into a sea of caramel. The losses were in the billions, the tens of billions. He refolded the paper (now costing two dollars) and asked for the check.

When he opened the envelope at home he could see that the principal amount was down three thousand, maybe four. Negligible, especially on a six-figure account. Still, the newspapers had him worried. People were getting loans for million-dollar homes while being gardeners, Mariachi singers. People's cleaning ladies, Appalachians and H'mong were starting out in converted war cottages and then flipping them, building waterfront spreads in Mingo Junction and the other river towns.

When the second statement arrived at the end of August, he took it out to a back porch table, where sparrows and red squirrels made strange, mechanical-looking movements in the unmowed grass. He'd been on his way to the shooting range in Covington (Kentucky state law was looser—you could carry the clip in the car with you) when the mail arrived early. He warmly greeted the letter carrier, a man of about his age with a thick West Virginia accent, clearly a civil service lifer. Carothers wondered if the man owned his own home, or was planning to now in the credit-rich, rising tide.

Anticipating something, he'd brought three phones out to the table, two handsets and a cell. He opened the envelope with his Swiss Army Knife. The account had gone down twelve thousand. A cold, blue ache went through his teeth. He held onto the table as if at a carnival ride, a small bead of perspiration gathering above his left eyebrow. He felt crippled, assaulted, even more so when the first handset didn't work. It was as if, in losing that first phone, he'd lost a line of defense, however symbolic, against the financial mysteries.

Lefferts' secretary put Carothers straight through to the broker.

Before Lefferts could say hello Carothers said "We've got to talk."

"Of course," said Lefferts. Carothers was put off by his cool, the low, business as usual purr of the man's baritone.

"You getting other callers, I assume?" he asked Lefferts.

"No more than usual," said the broker. Which was supposed to mean what? No more than was usual in an impending downturn? In an impending crisis? Or no more than usual when things were usual, or not unusual?

They made an appointment to meet at Wally's, in Mt. Adams. Trying to calm himself down, Carothers remembered their exemplary bourbon collection.

"Kind of shit happens all the time," said Lefferts. "Remember '87?"

"This big? No way" said Carothers. "It was a sell-off and a minor blip in the scheme of things. The market was back within two and a half months." He was spinning his napkin around in a circle.

Lefferts spread his hands. "It was huge. Absolutely whole fortunes lost. You gotta take some lumps. You gotta remember the important things. I was going in that week for thyroid cancer."

Carothers resented him playing the sympathy card, at least this soon.

"One good reason," he said, "I shouldn't put this into something safer."

"And what would that be?" Lefferts asked. "Goddam real estate? As if your first home isn't under water by now."

Carothers stopped with the napkin. "It's paid for. I'd like to keep it."

Lefferts seemed chastened for a moment, knowing he'd thrown out a line meant for younger clients.

"Of course it's paid for," he said.

Lefferts leaned forward toward Carothers, his eyes misting suddenly. "You've got bonds up the wazoo, no risk in those. And your equity portfolio is majorly conservative. Like one of the most conservative I've ever seen. Car, ride it out—we all are."

Again the eyes, the plea for sympathy.

Carothers waited for Lefferts to reach for the tab, making sure he'd pay. "Let's watch things," he said. "If it doesn't get better, we'll shake off some stocks."

Lefferts nodded. When his extended hand came up, Carothers looked at it for a second before shaking.

"Long haul," Lefferts said. "As Mr. Buffet likes to say. Long haul."

Carothers left wondering why Lefferts had turned his métier from smugness to helplessness, and saw it as further proof these people would try anything—that they were the worst of salesmen, the absolute bottom of the trough. They sold the most opaque, unstructured products in the world—things with no more real substance than a jellyfish—and yet the entire financial universe rested on them in lieu of a real foundation. Forget land. Forget services. All that was left now were these spineless, wriggling, insubstantial phantoms. What's more, at least this was what he was reading, the larcenous little devices no longer related to anything else, but only (presumably) to one another. Trillions and trillions of dollars resting on rows of digits reflecting only themselves, like little mirror fugues, with the average investor like himself helpless to understand them.

He realized a game of mathematics and business school lingo mixed together into a deadly gumbo, something only a handful of Ph.D modelers at certain investment banks could unravel. People like Lefferts had no more comprehension of it than anyone else, but were the gatekeepers, the fly-shooers, the soldiers of Oz making certain no one peeked behind the curtain. Still, he saw Lefferts as somebody who knew just enough to take a sort of secret glee in the vertiginous slipperyness with which the numbers rolled over everybody, humiliating them with confusion before ripping their financial life to pieces. It gave Carothers a new appreciation for the varieties of human pleasure and contempt.

* * *

Around the time he knew the third quarter statement was in the mail, he went to the range to calm himself. As the economy dove, crime rose, bringing more and more unlikely people to the narrow, blasting spaces, the alleys with their fluttering paper targets of ringed and numbered torsos. Who knows, thought Carothers, the joint might soon be taking the place of the golf course as wealth's mighty, abiding citadel. The tension eased out of him with the double-taps of the trigger, the muzzle flash and hefty, always surprising recoil. He could see people—men he really wouldn't want to know—ramping up their anger with such an exercise. But for him it had the opposite effect. The more thunder and fire that poured out of him, the more tranquil he became.

Still, in his awareness that even the smallest errors here could result in unimaginable horrors, in bathtubs of blood, he kept with the thought of the charge he could get from danger, the hints it would send out to him from beyond its curtain of heat. He first felt it when his father had driven his 9-year-old self straight past a highway patrol roadblock in Sun Valley, into the white heaven of a blizzard that had risen like a heedless creature out of the sunset. Their Austin creeped with terrible, tentative uncertainty, his father wiping the inside of the windshield with his fist, his voice quivering. The pounding of his young heart was fearsome, certainly, but at the same time it flooded his chest like a warm thick spilled drink, evening out with a new-found narcotic splendor.

The presence of women gave him the same charged sense of disequilibrium: their smells, their voices, everything about them. It started when he sat down next to the pep club girls in high school: all that decorum, the coy phrases and angora sweaters, and behind it all a force, something ineluctably powerful and invisible. Where was that charge now? Where in his life was there anything like that?

His task now was to carry on and preserve what he and his wife had built: stewarding that portfolio was his testament to her, the vehicle of her remaining presence. Danger was a memory, a sweet, missed ghost.

The new statement showed his principal to have fallen twenty percent. The anger rose in prickles under the skin beneath his hair. His hands trembled. The account number was still obscured, the initial Xs marching like invading, jackbooted soldiers.

He called Lefferts, brooking no excuses from him for being unavailable. He'd be at his office in an hour. Carothers' heart pounded on the drive over, in rhythm to the pavement separations of the freeway. He hoped it was Lefferts' golf day. Then his enmity ratcheted down a notch and he hoped it wasn't.

"What the hell happened?" Carothers stood in his doorway after the receptionist waved him through. It looked like his girl had been letting panicked people barge in like this all day.

"What do you mean what happened?" Lefferts was spinning through his rolodex.

"What do you mean 'What do you mean what happened?' I'm a quarter down. A deuce and a quarter off, governor."

Carothers had the statement in his hands, folded into three sections, and shoved it toward the broker. "This is completely unacceptable. You dipped me in shit here."

"This is happening to everybody. It happened quickly. It's nobody's fault."

"What coulda happened quickly is that you coulda bought a bond. It only takes a minute to buy a bond.This is what I pay you to do, to sit here all day and watch. You have the ticker, you have the Bloomberg screens."

"Jacky, the whole thing shifted. In an instant. It was like a seismic fault."

"It was like a what?" Carothers said, tapping the paper. "What the fuck IS this?"

Lefferts picked the paper up again and held it a second, two seconds. He ripped it in half, perfectly, as if along a perforation.

"Not important. Ignore it." Carothers gaped at him. "The whole harbor went down, every boat. And it will come back up, as sure as the sun will rise in the morning."

"How? And I don't buy all this ships sinking line. You could have pulled me out of more techs. Spread it around a little."

"I can't move it that fast. I can't foresee."

Carothers was still standing. He heard the door behind him creak. The secretary was checking in.

Carothers made a cross-cut motion with his hands. "You can

execute trades in an instant now. It's all computerized."

"Jack," Lefferts said, "The account is a safe one. Even the ironclad blue chips took a hit this time. It's awful, I know. But it's a temporary awful. It won't be awful in a year, two years, when you need it."

Carothers moved toward him. His fists clenched and released.

"I need..."

Lefferts was waiting. He started, ever so slowly, almost imperceptibly, to shake his head again.

"I need it now," Carothers said.

The phone buzzed. Carothers saw his watch out of the corner of his eye. It had seemed five minutes, ten minutes. But almost half an hour had gone by.

He had to give the appearance of composure, to let Lefferts know this wasn't his only game. He stepped back.

"What I mean to say is...I may need it now." He stared at the torn statement, smoothing the front of his shirt with his hands. Then he turned and walked out.

Carothers tried to control his despair in the following weeks. Basically, this entailed going to the range, and drinking. Sometimes he did both, indulging in the latter first, and noticed that the only leeway it allowed him was carrying a full magazine in the trunk, technically a misdemeanor, and sneaking a few reloads in, also already packed, their gleaming metal jackets lined up like columns in a tiny golden temple.

Carothers thought often of his wife in these days. He imagined her sitting, watching him, not on a throne of clouds or anything celestial, but simply in the stuffed blue Pierre Deux chair that had been one of their last few luxuries before their retirement. As the days wore on and his worry over their dwindling nest increased, her eyes lost none of their recent remembered luster, but simply narrowed, trimmed themselves with scrutiny. He saw her just like that, perfectly, facing him in the same room and picking at the pleats of her skirt.

* * *

In the last days of January, the fourth quarter statements arrived with colored packets of coupons from Home Depot (weren't they going under?) and a solitary notice of delinquent parking ticket from the Cincinnati Police Department. The mail was late and it was close enough to four for Carothers to pour himself a bourbon. The amber liquid splashed around the column of ice like fountain water, rising in bubbled silence to even itself over the highest cube. Carothers lifted the glass and let it sting his lips. Outside, a pair of cardinals circled one another, skipping and jumping, the black crinkles of their eyes and wing tips thrown up like cinders in the whirl of red.

He took another drink, fingering the lone remaining envelope. He picked it up and held it against the window's light, but couldn't see anything but the companion logo of the wholesale brokerage house.

He opened it, keeping his eyes closed, taking a third drink.

His principal was down $37,000. Darkness closed in from the corners of his eyes, but he moved the chair and walked the two long strides to the French doors and put his head against the chilly, small square of glass. The birds were gone. The fumes of the liquor ignited behind his eyes, in his chest, down through his shoulders and extended arms.

A day or two before he had read about brokers "front-running" stocks on their customers. When a client placed an order to a broker to buy stock X at a certain price, the broker would buy those shares for its own portfolio ahead of the customer's order. If the stock's price rose, the broker kept the increase for himself. If the value fell, he fobbed them off into the customer's account. There were new revelations about the rating agencies, old, august entities that Carothers' father used to mention when reading the financial pages. They were supposed to be objective, arms-length assessments by companies separate from those issuing securities. But in reality the issuing firms were paying the raters to do their rating. It was like a theater paying a newspaper to give a good review of its play.

He went down to the car. As he opened the trunk and threw in his jacket he saw that the pistol lay on one side, propped by the wheel hump in its Kevlar case, and the clip lay on the other side, in a freezer bag that occluded the shine of its cartridges.

He pulled into the packed parking lot, figuring others had made the same discoveries, read the same stories, made the same connections. Amazingly, both the receptionist and secretary's desks were empty, and Carothers barged forward, taking from one of their desks a sheet of paper he intended to pass off as his own statement.

He tapped on the door. Then he pushed it open.

Lefferts was getting up and putting folders in his briefcase. He looked at Carothers with a blank expression, unafraid and only slightly startled. "Car—what's up? Lucy buzz you in?"

"No, Lucy didn't buzz me in. What happened this time?" He lifted the paper up, ticking its folded length back and forth like a metronome. "I'm sucking wind here."

"Car, we've been through this. Everybody's feeling it. Everybody's fighting."

"Did everybody know about these fronting schemes? Did you? Did you try a little of that stuff?"

Lefferts looked down at the partitions in his valise. He shook his head. "I've got an appointment, Car. I really need to go."

He wouldn't meet Carothers' eyes. He snapped the briefcase shut and walked toward a door at the side of his office, a door Carothers always thought was a bathroom but which now proved to be another exit, an escape route, he imagined, for situations the broker had long foreseen.

Carothers leapt at him and grabbed his jacket.

"Car! What in the hell?"

Carothers brought his other arm around to catch the hand Lefferts had lifted to shoo off his grip.

"Where you going? Off to place some orders for yourself?"

"I don't have to listen to this shit, Car."

He was through the door and into the foyer Carothers had never seen before, but which he noticed had a windowed door to the back parking lot. Expensive cars stood outside. Lefferts' Jaguar, an effeminate pastel blue, was parked with its rear to the curb. Carothers had Lefferts' collar in the tight grip of his right hand. He'd dropped the secretary's document.

Lefferts lurched back and forth, swinging the briefcase at Carother's arms, trying to shake out of his jacket. When he grabbed the knob of the outer door he turned around, his face glistening with red blotches and sweat.

"What in the fuck are you doing, John? Let go of me."

The secretary was behind them now, announcing in a piping, eerily calm voice that she had called security.

The door flew open and its spring hinge flung it back at Carothers, smashing him in the face. But it was Lefferts that fell outside, collapsing like a stage clown on the perfectly clean blacktop. Carothers, the metallic tinge of blood filling his mouth, stood above him and felt below his jacket for the knobby stock of the pistol. But there were footsteps behind him now, and a police car pulled into the parking lot with a single, gulping whoop that filled the winter air like a thunderclap.

Carothers got down on his knees, faking a pain in his stomach, and when he was sure no one behind or in front of him could see, especially not Lefferts, he slipped the gun out of his belt and slid it across the ground into a storm drain. More blood came out of his mouth, out of his nose and ears, and then there was blackness.

Carothers sat at his kitchen table, the icepack held to his face, the tight red handcuff indentations still visible on his wrists. There were four new pieces of paper on his table, wobbling together in his distorted sight, shimmering and fluttering at him like paper targets through the throbs and flashes of pain.

The City of Cincinnati had rejected his attempt to charge the parking ticket to a Visa account, noting the issuer had indicated the card was no longer valid. The second was a notice from the Unified School District that he had been selected to receive a commendation for his long tenure as a principal, and indeed would be honored as one of three outstanding school administrators in the system's previous quarter century. The third was a receipt for nominal bail of $250 for an assault booking, Queen's County Police, posted by check from the offices of Edward Lefferts Brokerage, LLC, member, New York Stock Exchange and NASDAQ.

The fourth pile was really a small stack of onion skin pages that had arrived in an 8 1/2 by 11 manila envelope. It was from the American Funds Group and was covered by a letter of apology for having sent him statements that in fact were those of another investor. The letter went on to express regret at a confusion of social security and account numbers, and particularly apologized for the fact that his actual losses were far less severe than those of his mis-digited doppelganger.

Bourbon was such a blessed thing, thought Carothers. No anesthetic or analgesic could deliver an equivalent oblivion, and he recalled that many years ago, when he was still teaching history before his principalship, he enjoyed the fact that Union Army surgeons would give the battle-wounded the option of a Kentucky cask draw over an injection of morphine. His left hand held the compresses while his right hand poured.

Outside, in the falling snow, he expected to see the image of Alice again. But he didn't. She remained invisible as she often had in life, after errors of his so great she could only absent herself to signal forgiveness. All there was through the window now, inside the large, soft bandage-white snowflakes, were the two cardinals—blood-red and bruise-black—going into their terrible, brilliant twirl.

Flatlanders

"Some around here may say some things. Some around here." Rajiv looked away.

"Some around here. You know that."

Rajiv ran the back of his hand across his beard.

"But not most. And not me."

Rajiv looked back at him. Their eyes locked in an even, easeful trust.

Gale was what the Texan said his name was. It struck Rajiv as a feminine name. But many Indian names were odd to Americans, and certainly to Texans. Other immigrants who had settled here, shopkeepers of a lower level, not Indians but Bengalis, had names of long, choppy syllables. Rajiv himself could not guess where to place the stress in such proper nouns, how to work the elisions.

The Texan went back to how the mortgages on his fellow merchants' stores had a fatal tail effect that still lay "in the grass" now six years after the crash of 2008. Many, Gale said, had gotten loan modifications for their warehouses, "mods" was the shorthand, but many had not been able to qualify. Many warehouse owners were too busy trying to save their homes to do a workout on a commercial space, so they had to fall behind on the business mortgage. One or two lost their inventory space, and had to lease from Gale.

Rajiv looked out to the parking lot. Here in Texas, so much of what a man was was in the driveway. Gale's large black pick-up stood in the row of broken down mini-trucks and vans.

Rajiv looked back from the pebble clouds of the lot into Gale's steel-blue eyes. He ignored the sounds of arriving motorcycles.

He ignored the further thoughts of how a race of men could be born with eyes as blue as Gale's. In Varanasi, only gods had eyes that blue. In the Ganges Valley, only the otherworldly—not that Rajiv believed any of it—had features that vivid and striking.

Gale leaned forward as the bikers came in. Rajiv noticed the old saddlebags on the Harleys, filled with magazines, large rolled-up maps or blueprints, red sticks that looked like batons relay runners handed to one another at the high school track near Rajiv's house.

Gale put the brow of his nose into his joined fingers. Bikers called out to him, and he waved absently, not looking their way.

"Roger," Gale said (Rajiv had liked the Anglicization), "I want you to know people are hurting here. Hell, I don't need to tell you that."

Rajiv nodded.

"Somebody like you that came here flush..." He winced at the choice of words. "Someone who has more stability, more flow, is going to get hit up for help by your fellow citizens."

Gale winked.

"They can't afford to lease equipment, some of them. They might want to borrow drill parts, bits, generators."

Rajiv nodded, leaning back in his chair at what he thought would come next.

But there was no next. Gale simply wanted him to know of the expectation, and that it wasn't any kind of threat.

"I would be happy to help," said Rajiv. "If they could just sign a ledger, tell them..."

Rajiv's father had been a colonel in the Yemeni Air Force. There was never a payment, never the event of a transaction, without a receipt, an entry on a ledger.

"No, no," Gale's hands went up as he brushed this away. His palms were open, like a man being held up. "Don't even think of parting with a can of 1040 without a receipt. Don't even think."

Rajiv nodded. More cars were pulling up to the diner. Gale said it would be a rough ride, a sad ride for some of their fellow quip leasors and warehousemen. He said that with teamwork—a word Rajiv had learned from American football—everybody would do fine. But Rajiv should expect a little more borrowing than usual.

Gale stared straight ahead above Rajiv's eyes, to the spot where a Brahmin dot would appear if Rajiv were a woman.

"Roger, let me ask you something else. You work yourself to death in this place. You and the wife and girls. I think all of you need a break."

Rajiv thought hard about evenings he would claim to be busy, but of course there were none. All evenings were empty in an empty place.

"All people, you know all countries have their dancing. You. Your country. Us."

Gale unfolded his hands. "We square dance here. I'd like you to see the kind of stuff we do. You wouldn't have to dance. But the ladies?..."

How did he, Gale, know a Muslim man could not dance in public?

"Saturday nights," Rajiv said, "are difficult for us."

The bikers raised their voices. One of them at the next table mentioned Gale's name.

"Well," Gale said, "There'll be lots of boys. And lots of Dads like you to keep an eye on."

Gale's voice descended knowingly. Rajiv didn't have to guess that he had daughters.

Rajiv wanted an end to all of this: the assessments, the assurances, the promise of watchfulness, if not safety.

The bikers were leaving silently, dragged down by their liquor. Rajiv put his hands on the table, folded them together in the strange grip of these people's prayers.

"I accept," he said, before Gale could even smile.

At the house, his daughters both hugged him. They wore shorts with simple tops and no veils, and Awah, his wife, was visible in the kitchen with her mouth cover unsnapped and the rest of the hijab pulled back from her hair.

When they sat down to dinner, without the slightest thought of how he would bring it up, he simply told them of the invitation. The girls stopped chewing and looked at him. Fatima, the youngest, said she saw him so little now, with drilling going on, that she didn't want to only be able to sit beside him at a dance with people they didn't know.

"They are our neighbors, our community. For now. It is an invitation, and from an important man, this Gale."

A glow of curiosity came into their eyes. The wariness remained—the gestures of their mouth and hands.

He knew attire would be a sticking point. They knew he knew. An Arab woman can read a man's mind.

"They can wear jeans. But they can keep the hijab on by itself," he said. Conspiracy and hedging hung in their faces like shadows.

"We can think of something," Ahma, the oldest, said. "It's not like the kids haven't seen us unveiled."

Rajiv wondered exactly what to make of this. Was it a hint of something sexual, some adventure? Had they walked around the halls at times with no headgear at all?

"Will you be there the whole time?" Ahma asked him.

"You were just saying how you never saw me." She reiterated, staring. He knew what she meant.

He smiled. "I will stay lost with the rest of the men. I promise I will if you come. The rest I leave to your Mom."

The mother's mood had darkened. She eked out a panicked smile. He had not seen her like this since the last cluster of days before leaving Yemen. Skin darkening with blush. Lips curling. Eyes white as oblivion.

He gathered it wasn't the absence from her country that saddened her. It wasn't the utter, sheer lunacy of the place they were in. It wasn't the queasiness of not knowing, really not knowing what the town felt about them. It was something else. He prayed often that it was not him.

She put the tabbouleh plate in the sink, letting it slip from her hands so that it cracked loudly. A fleck of green—a kernel or a leaf—flew up and stuck to her face.

It was still late afternoon as they drove to the vets lodge for the square dance. Everything in front of the car wavered, wobbled in the heat. There were not sizeable deserts in Yemen and one had to cross over the sea into Saudi territory to see genuine heat and sand like this; hallucinatory, Rajiv thought: things flickering, waiting for long moments like living creatures, then changing into something else.

He glanced at his wife, staining the air with her eyes. Her face only relaxed at the sound of the girls fighting in back—slaps on the window, lame judo chops.

The drive to the lodge had seemed long to Rajiv, something with the atmosphere of empty highways, vast distances full of waste and loss. But inside the air was warm with music—high, bright fiddles and the happy plunk of fretted instruments. The band was on the stage and a man stood at the microphone, speaking quickly like a price caller Rajiv had seen once at an equipment auction. After introductions, Gale escorted them forward into the sea of red and white, cloth-covered tables.

Awah was fascinated with the women's dresses. They were flouncy, yellow or red or brown pastel, with some underdress that flared them out like shaking bells.

They sat down at the table Gale directed them to. There were two couples; both men were equipment dealers like Rajiv, and one's wife was a teacher, the other's a nurse.

"Owen," one of the men leaned over to shake hands with Rajiv. He introduced his wife, Hazel, to Awah. Blanche was the other wife's name and her husband, Travis, introduced her and one of the daughters. They said the other was out dancing. Awah could not take her eyes off the clothes, the dance clothes. Owen had a jacket with odd, flaring lapels and a tie that looked like shoestrings joined at the top by a piece of turquoise. Some of the men out on the floor wore what Awah once called cowboy hats, but was corrected to say "western" hats.

The music was joyful. Like some Yemeni music, and the music of the Sufis, Awah heard it as a kind of sound of the heart itself, its own boundless, limitless cry of joy. The Sufis thought music's source was separate from the mind and even the soul—that it was the signature of a temperament, a good or bad temperament, whichever way it was shaped by a union with God. And like the dervishes, that union could only be ecstatic, barely controllable, full of clamor and sparkle and flash.

The steps of the square dance were hard to follow at first. Awah was used to the isolation of an individual Sufi dancer. But this dancing was all groups and rows, lines that broke open and changed direction. Partners would switch with the orders of the caller, and a "do-see-do" meant a whirl around your partner, who you would rejoin in a move called a "promenade," a reunion which brought the entire group marching together again.

Awah had studied mathematics in Lahore, and the dancing made her think of geometry, of lines and circles and angles.

Rajiv was being asked questions by Travis, all about business, the difficulty of it, the absence of it.

"We need a good long string of hits on these leases," Travis said, leaning forward with a cigar.

Rajiv declined, agreeing, while Travis unwrapped his own Monte Cristo.

"Don't mean to be prying. Nothing personal," said the Texan. "But I was wondering where your…your seed money came from."

He spit out the bit-off end.

"Your people, before they went to Yemen, do well there in India?"

Rajiv noted the pronunciation, which could have been taken negatively, but decided not to. Travis seemed innocent enough. As helpless, in the face of things, as most of the others.

"Telephones, yes. It is a spread-out country. Not as much as yours. But telephones were needed."

Travis nodded with only a hint of a smile.

"We supplied," said Rajiv, reaching for his ice water.

"All business we welcome here. Anyone, from anywhere. But there are some here who, you know…" Travis scanned the window frames, weighing the point he was about to make. "You folks, not exactly from here…Some of the people here, wanting you to succeed of course. Well, they just want you to do it sort of quietly."

Rajiv looked straight at him.

"They want you to succeed along with everybody. Not so much out ahead of 'em."

Rajiv, a little angry, felt the crossness turn in a strange new direction. He thought of himself, and how he had disappointed people here by getting on accounts the others might have been lucky enough to get. The disappointments he had handed to people, from all manners of attention or inattention on his side, seemed like small things inside of him, rattling around inside his body, like those little

Russian dolls. He, too, seemed like one of the dolls, fallen over in a corner of that space, trapped beneath the others.

Awah's mood had brightened again. The dancers had switched to something called the Two-Step. She sat on the edge of her seat to watch. This was a slower, statelier dance, less formal, less geometric and having less steps. The man twirled his partner and then held her at arm's length, pausing and gazing at her.

Gale turned around to look at this. It seemed to be one of his favorite dances. When people still sitting at the tables clapped, Awah clapped too, louder and louder as the music rose.

Their daughters had joined in this most Texan of dances, moving closely with their clumsy, earnest boy partners, standing at arm's length with mock coy looks, then shrieking at the suddenness of being twirled.

There was a crucial step in the dance that involved the couple making a square with their hands and arms, which looked to Rajiv to be a difficult move. The square was a window, the frames of their sun-browned arms surrounding invisible glass. They looked through it at one another and smiled, relishing their boundary, relishing the access of sight to the other.

When the window was dismantled and the dancers rejoined one another, their bodies pressing together, Rajiv saw that Awah's smile was one of contentment, of safety, an assurance—after all these doubtful months—that here the stranger could be cherished, as children are cherished, simply for being themselves.

The dancers bowed to the audience when they stopped. Their daughters stood between their partners, looking out to their parents. Fatima smiled, her sister smiling but keeping her newly orthodontured mouth clamped shut. Awah wiped her eyes with the hijab.

The arms of the dancers stayed lifted, intertwined, like the intersecting thatches of a shelter curving around against the wind and waste of what lay outside the building. Their hands reached over to others who were not their partners, their giggles rising, their limbs crossing and thickening until it became just that—a laughing, circled wall lit up by itself, by its own blind light of homecoming.

Out on the night horizon, the white blobs of light floated and curdled like spoiled cream refusing to dissolve. Their failure to merge into a single stream dividing road and sky gave Rajiv a premonition of wrongness, of mistaken direction. But of course they were going the only way they could, on the main highway back to the Midland suburbs. Awah was asleep. The girls were getting there, punching one another into slumber.

The outer parts of the city began to surround them: familiar, concentric circles of light. The Mexican neighborhoods were nestled between these and the warehouse district where his own space lay alongside those of his competitors. His business neighbors, as Gale had put it.

He had never heard American sirens before, only the clumsy whoop-whoop of the Yemeni magistrate's trishaws. So he didn't recognize the concave blasts of the fire trucks that were a couple blocks ahead of him now. He'd never seen emergency vehicles in the warehouse district, only dump trucks and backhoes putting up new buildings.

As he turned off the highway and into the street the passenger window lit up with an even light that then began to flicker and twist as he eased up on the gas and started to coast. There were fire trucks, rain-coated men, and above them a silvery cloud of the hose water's mist. Inside it, solid walls of flame licked up the sides of his building, bright red and orange, and inky smoke shot out of the roof in back of the angled lines of water and ladders. The wall nearest the street had begun collapsing. It sagged like the side of the Halloween pumpkin they'd left out on the porch too long.

He got out and stood in the street beside his open door. The bikers were in a side alley looking up at the flames. One of them tapped against his boot a stick like the one he'd seen in their saddlebags. When they saw him watching them they got on their bikes and rode away, swaying, weaving around one another.

He got the attention of one of the men, pointing to himself. Mine, his finger and his closed fist said. The firemen knew who he was. They were going to let him stay, but motioned him back into the car. He rested his cheek on the grooves of the steering wheel. His wife and daughters did not wake up. He watched their deep and even breathing as the shadows of the flames came through the windshield and passed over their faces.

The Wave Function

Professor Wollheim, a quantum physicist, had need of a new housekeeper and personal secretary. The last one had left to take care of her deteriorating mother, and gave only three or four days' notice. Though he felt some discomfort showing up on campus, given recent events and obscure allegations against his work, or his lack of a working team, or something, he rode his people-mover down to the bulletin board in the Union and posted, in black marker, a sign that said: PERSONAL ASSISTANT NEEDED; LIVE-IN; COMPUTER-SAVVY; COOK & CLEAN; NEATNESS A NECESSITY. His hands trembled as he sunk the push pins, bright orange, into the flesh-colored, crowded pressboard.

Ever since he'd had the TIA ("mini-stroke" one doctor called it) he found he couldn't move as fast, his hands had less control, not shaking so much as simply failing, giving out, dropping things. The forgetfulness bothered him more, increasing his dependence on other academics he'd regarded as less talented, less seasoned and polished, and less competitive, given that physics posts were in short supply and job security was more solid than it had been before the 9/11 hiring boom.

Professor Mana passed him in the hall, gave him what Woll regarded as a condescending pat. What was he doing here? In a student building? Wollheim was more used to seeing him at the faculty club, in conversational circles Wollheim was never invited into. Sometimes all of them were looking in his direction. Most were gracious, but there were one or two smiles that bordered on smirks.

Was it Nietzsche, Schopenhauer? Someone of that pessimist

ilk had thrown out an aphorism Wollheim woke to now in the mornings and often several times a night. When fate comes, it comes with both hands. The "peer review" of some of his work was faltering. Though most of his colleagues, at all colleges, worked mainly alone, tinkering alone in digital isolation or on sheets of foolscap, his findings were too close to those of other universities' departments to not give a suspicious tang to his latest papers. But he had worked on the issue—the collapse of the wave function—as long as they had, as imaginatively and thoroughly, and beginning—though these days it could work against you—before some of them were born.

"Wollheim," said a loud voice at his back. He turned to see Yellen, a trustworthy colleague, one who always seemed to freely give of what was asked of him.

"How you feeling?"

"Better," Wollheim said, "a good bit better. Thanks."

"I saw your sign. Mary has someone she knows, someone from choir."

Wollheim leaned back against the wall, put his hands down into the deep pockets of his khakis, "You vouch for her?"

"Oh Bill, she's great. A dependable contralto."

Wollheim smiled, worked his eyes up toward the ceiling.

"A little eccentric, very intense. Very diligent."

"Send her over," said Wollheim. "Give her my cell and we'll set something up."

* * *

His phone, he hated these things, was ringing as he pulled into his drive. It was her.

"Professor Wollheim?" Her voice was pitched higher than a contralto's. More like a soprano, one who could tremelo through the most warbling of arias.

"I could come, could come…could…I could be there between five and six. Don't want, don't want to interfere with any family dinner, or family dinner, I was…"

"Don't have a family," he said, in the tone of a rebuke. "Can you find your way to the Aquatic Park cul-de-sacs?"

"Yes, I'm at the Divisadero Mall now. I'll GPS."

He gave her directions and noticed the halting and repetition in her speech again. When she hung up he wondered at its high register, her stuttering, the echoes of getting the clotted words out. He held the phone away at arm's length. He had the idea that these features of her speech were something laying in the device itself, like one of its things or sudden lights.

She was thin and short, almost dwarfish. As he pulled in he thought she was speaking to one of the bushes. She later explained, when her keys were on the table and they'd sat down, that the bushes could use a trim.

Describing the work she'd done for others, she allowed herself to slow down some. She talked as her mother had talked, the kind of chatter that comes from keeping a pot of coffee on the burner all day. She'd put on one of her hippie caftans, one of those British things one of her fellow vocalists called by some Arab or Berber name. Looking around the house, seeing its absence of monitors and yellow pads, she knew immediately it needed organizing, that organization was everything to him, one of those kinds of people with one of those minds.

"Nothing is ever misplaced," she said. "I do not lose things," she added. "I keep clients' premises much cleaner than my own. Not that mine is dirty—I'm just so seldom there."

"But I know," she said after a pause, "that order is the essence of things. Especially for a man of your abilities. Your discipline and your abilities."

He stared at her.

"Your work," she said.

She stared at him as though she were looking through him, at the lightening of the sun on the wall.

"I'm sure, sure, sure I can do it, Professor." She reached into her bag, also something North African, and pulled out a sheet of references.

"Any one of these people could..."

He raised his hand.

"Start in the morning?"

Her eyes widened under the squiggly, nervous wires of her hair.

"Oh Professor, that would be lovely."

That night as he drifted off, tided into the Ambien haze his doctors had prescribed as the data scandal grew, he felt good about her energy, the sparkle and zest of it. He liked the intensity of the old hippie-dippiness, its uplifting velocity. He had a sense she could keep the piles clear and separated, that she could give the place some unoverwhelmed emptiness and peace. And there he would be able to gather himself—however he might be failing—for what now seemed to be the fight of his life.

Greta loved to keep her hands busy even when they were not attending to the professor. She doodled and drew on small pads she brought from Staples, and wrote friends—old-fashioned letters, none of the e-mail stuff—she had kept from caregiving facilities elsewhere. She loved crosswords, keeping them folded into squares and slid neatly down into her apron pockets, and leaving them sometimes laying on top of his own stacks of work. When this happened she chided herself, tsk-tsking without saying anything more as she lifted the squared newspaper away from his strange materials.

She was shaming and correcting herself, her bushy hair swaying, one afternoon when she found a pad of her squiggly drawings laying in front of his shelf of German physics texts. She was particularly upset with herself that day, dissatisfied with her mistake. It was a hot September afternoon more like midsummer than the chill that would be coming in an Indian Summer. She remembered it being called that from her childhood, her aunts would say *We're having an Indian Summer here aren't we?*

Just as she was lifting the drawing she heard his stockinged feet and a second or two later the waft of his stinking breath floating over the papers. She didn't look around when he asked her where she had come from, what her name was. He asked her how long she would be staying with him.

She looked down at the drawings as if they were something else, then turned around slowly, her hands fidgeting with the papers, and said: Why Professor, I did not know you had forgotten my name. It is Greta. I come from the Service. And I suppose, if it is OK with you, and we work out OK, I'll be here as long as I'm needed.

One night Professor Wollheim sat Greta down and told her

about quantum mechanics. She sunk deep in her chair, and ran her almost uncontrollably busy fingers along the ridge the cushion made with the side board of the chair, so he couldn't see. She said she remembered Newton, but when he raised his hand she knew she was in for something splendidly new. He said that one of his predecessors' discoveries was that light, which had long been thought by some to be particles and by others to be waves, could form small beams or ripples that played through the spaces of dark air like the old movie searchlights. He told her at one point the particles were so thick that they took on, out of the sumptuous negation that surrounded them, a mass of their own that would waver and coarsen like a grainy sort of soup, and at that point the particles just collapsed—that's the word he stressed—into waves. It was this that was called the wave function, or the collapse of the wave packet. Her hands moved along the ridge of the aging fabric and she finally brought them up, joining them together like praying hands so they would not look too busy. She pushed them toward him in a thrust of appreciation.

"My stars," she said. "That is just the most amazing thing. Is everything that you study this exciting?"

He rested his head in the high-pillowed chair and told her to put out one of her fingers. The look on his face was amused, but in a sinister, almost grisly way, and he asked her if she would be surprised to know if the atoms, the atoms and parts of atoms in her hands, could have a relationship—relationship, he stressed the word—with the atoms in something far away, perhaps a universe far away?

Her eyes widened.

"That would indeed surprise me. And how would you know it, Professor? How could it be proved?"

He smiled, wider now, the darkness leaving his face.

"That," he said, "is for the next lesson."

The next lesson was on a day when her hands were so nervous they seemed to be flying everywhere, like small animals you kick up in the grass and get away before you can tell what they are. For a while they kept busy arranging tiny things on his desk—marbles, paperweights, objects bought in expensive German-named stores in Union Square, long black boxes with what looked like beams inside them and which she knew had something to do with his science but were more like decorative toys or games. Outside, the Professor was standing in what had before been a lush interior garden but now, in the drought, was a drooping cross-hatch of brown shrubs and barkless eucalyptus. His own hands, too, were busy, but in a slower, more thoughtful way. Thoughts were all that occupied him now—that or forgetfulness, the new gaps she had noticed in his memory. He stood against a tree, his hand braced against it. He ran his hand up and down the slick trunk and when his spread palm stopped at a spot he began talking to himself, caressing the tree as he muttered. He frowned as he babbled, the dark, pin-sharp edge of his mouth fallen downward.

When he came in and she said "I wanted to tell you, Professor, how much I enjoyed our talk the other day," he slumped into the guest chair in front of his desk and took the cue to begin talking physics again, begin trying to get through to her how it was the narrative structure of the world, the picture of all possible forms of reality itself. He didn't expect her to understand but took it as practice once all the idea theft and plagiarism blew over and he might be invited back for an emeritus lecture, a 'short course' they called them now.

He smiled at her condescendingly, joining the tips of his two fingers together in front of his nose. She grabbed one of her hands, twitching now, in the palm of the other, and kept both under the drop of her apron.

"Measurement," he said, "is everything in physics. Who measures. What's measured." He paused. "Is there something there at all if we don't measure it?"

He wasn't looking at her but over at the desk.

"What did you do?"

"Excuse me, Professor? I was straightening for you. Tidying."

His skin blushed more like it had outside.

She needed to soften him and thought of a wedge she could enter with. "I redded it up. Isn't that the funniest word? It's a Midwesternism. Some German word, I think. To red, a verb. Like: 'red up the table.'"

"Don't move things," he said. "Dust around them but don't move…"

He stopped.

"Gladys," he said, "DON'T move."

"Oh Professor, I apologize."

"Gladys, don't ever move anything."

"Professor, my apologies. And you must have forgotten my name. My name is Greta."

He looked at her with a mixture of fury and blankness.

"Greta," he said.

"So, measurement," she cued him to continue.

"Greta, how did you get here?" He twisted in his chair, staring at her, clutching his hands on its arms like a man adrift on a log, in dark water.

When she came back in the room with tea he was slouched back down in the chair, watching the fire. She laid his saucer and spoon the way he liked it, separate from the cup. She sat down and crossed her fingers, running the tips of her nails over each knuckle, underneath the apron's trim.

"Measurement," she said. "We were going to talk about measurement."

He stared at her.

"There's no measurement any more, no calibration, no weighing. There's no assessment. There's no way to tell what anyone has achieved."

She turned her head into the angle of a question.

"All this," he said, pointing to the computers. "The discoveries, experiments. The work of it, whoever did it, belongs to everyone now."

She said she thought his achievements would certainly be, certainly were, credited to him, that there were patents and such, legal protections to give credit to the person who truly created whatever it was.

"I devised a thing or two," he said. "My T.A.s, my grad students took it elsewhere. Took it to new places. To businesses."

She made a "tsk" which she knew made her sound old.

"Gladys, when you reddened, redded, whatever you call it, what happened to the papers?"

"Why Professor, I put everything back where it was. I

wouldn't do anything, move anything."

His flesh was scarlet now, glistening.

"I certainly wouldn't remove anything."

The stare bore through her like a steel rod.

"How do I know," he asked, "that you didn't take something? One of the equation sets?"

"Professor, I wouldn't dream of anything like that. I put everything back in its place."

He stared.

"And please, call me Greta. I know it's sometimes hard to remember."

He rose up slightly, his body bending into an odd angle from his refusal to take his eyes off her.

"How know, how did I know you're not in with them?"

"With who, Professor?"

"With them," he said. "The students. You came from the school, the job boards."

Now he was rising up, wobbling, his hand reaching for his cane.

"Professor?" she said loudly, wanting to shout her resentment. When she looked down she saw that he'd spilled tea on the crotch of his pants.

"Let me get you to your room," she said. "You need a new pair of trousers."

He raised his hand as he had in his talks, but with the cane in one of them.

"Don't touch me."

Greta smoothed down the front of her apron and said she would simply steer him toward the door of his room.

"Don't touch me!" he said again. The saucer and spoon had now fallen to the floor.

"Who are you?" His voice was rising with each word. Beads of sweat, large drops, ran down the ridges of his nose and onto the end table. She saw the wetness pooling there.

She ran ahead of him and flicked on the light switch.

"Who are you?" he yelled.

"Professor, what's wrong? Let me take your arm and help you onto the bed. I'll get you fresh trousers from the closet."

Her hands were frantic. They struggled with the closet knobs.

"WHO ARE YOU?"

"Pajamas," she said. "What was I thinking? It's your pajama bottoms you need."

"I don't know you," he said, standing stone still, his back rigid now, his long finger in the air, crookedly pointing.

She went over to the pillows, the fresh pressed cases she'd ironed that morning.

"You're death," he yelled. "You are DEATH."

He would not sit down.

"I want to go home." He bent himself at the waist and then straightened again. "I want to be home."

"But Professor," she said calmly, smoothing the pillows with her suddenly calm hands. "You're home. You *are* home."

Yellow Jacket

The doorman kept sticking his head into the foyer as Jack's cab idled. The doors gleamed gold and mahogany brown, and the polish of the floor's marble sent the same light up into the house staff's faces. On the great oak table a bouquet of astromeria and Calla lilies spread up into the air, each stem and blossom carefully studied and placed. Jack was sure it had its own attendant, coming forward from time to time with garden shears to make adjustments. Another man was sorting mail and yet another had an armful of coats that looked like a gathered and lifted animal.

The doorman came back out and lifted his finger to Jack. "Wait," was the message, "just one more minute."

Jack put his head back down into the paper, regarding with admiration the crispness of the Peter Pushbottom sweater ad. Stores had their preferred places for box kickers on the first two pages of the Times. It was 1978. The 80s seemed far off to Jack, but he read now, every day, projections of all kinds with end dates in the eighth numeral of the Century. The small saddlery and boot shop ads had sketched ivy twining up their borders, and the breeze in the open window blew them, along with the rest of the paper, up into his face.

Jack's head was still down when Kissinger got into the back seat. The doorman was doing something with an umbrella and a satchel, steering the portly man into place on the fake black leather of the rear of the car.

Jack looked into the rearview. The statesman's jaws were enormous, like a bulldog's. They were slightly pockmarked, traces of suffering he'd endured at the hands of his fellow gymnasium students back in Dortmund. "Truculent" was the word that came to Jack's mind, from the description of the dead priest's face in Joyce's "The Sisters." Jowls like a mastiff's. Churchillian. Dr. K would have enjoyed the comparison.

"Take the Drive down to 140 Broadway, exit Pearl," the Teutonic bass instructed. "I usually take Broadway all the way down but the President is in town, UN." Both "President" and "UN" were tinctured with distaste.

Jack turned his Checker west out of the River House's carriage drive, south onto York Avenue. The jagged spurs and cables of the Queensboro Bridge flaked green paint out into the wind. Falling apart, Jack thought. The fucking city is falling apart.

When the older man saw more blocks of surface streets, he renewed his request that Jack take the Drive. He pulled onto it at 42nd Street. Sure enough, as soon as the cab's tires took on the elevated, flabby grab of asphalt, Jack saw the doctor's eyes sneering in the rearview at the U.N's blue-green flank of eastern windows. The river was filled with whitecaps, tilting buoys, and one barge looking long enough to land a plane on, misted with flocks of hungry gulls.

Jack got off the FDR using the acronymed route he learned in the hack exam: PWW, Pearl to Water to Wall. Bond Street brought him up to the giant orange tube sculpture at 140 Broadway. The great man knew he would be recognized here, and suddenly grew a hat and tinted, snap-on lenses. He gave Jack a fifty dollar bill, and into the passenger's hand Jack returned a twenty and five ones. The great man let him keep a dollar bill. It looked oddly small in Jack's palm, like the tiny bills Reagan was holding up in campaign speeches, calling them "Carter dollars."

Jack had been driving three months, deciding which professional school exam to take: the GMAT, the LSAT, the Accountancy Entrance. The stories he had been sending out to little magazines—their addresses cribbed in the Gotham Book Mart's journal room—had come back like tiny, stinging boomerangs. He'd failed the typing test at publishers, so the editorial assistant route was vanishing. Hacking gave him freedom, his own time, the mobility to fly through the city's giant, ever-promising night. Silence, cunning and exile all were fine, but he was hedging his bets, wanting to straddle two worlds like William Gaddis did—writing by starlight but during the day going into an office, wearing suits, understanding the brittle nomenclature of *The Wall Street Journal*.

The celebrities gave him something to write to his sisters about. Betty Friedan crossed in front of him at Central Park South, and Bernstein, at the gate of the Dakota, got out of what seemed a series of cars, his long white scarves floating. Bill Murray got into the car at St. Vincent's Hospital, and Jack took him to NBC Studios, where Saturday Night Live was riding the early, great crest of itself. Murray said Jack didn't look like a lifer, just a college boy, and after Jack gave him his change he asked Murray for "noogies," the small head lock and knuckle bang on the scalp that had become a show staple and that Jack's father, when giving them to his son as a child, had called a "dutch rub".

What impressed them most at home was his decline of the great First Lady, the truest world historical figure who had ever raised her hand for him to stop. He was actually stopped already, her hand rapping on his window where he had parked in the fashion district. He'd committed himself to a West Coast fur buyer for the day—a "horse hire"—and there she was, the face of the century, the smile and sparkling eyes that shifted him suddenly a decade and a half backwards—the slim, pink-skirted body stretched across the trunk of the car as the secret service agent pushed her down into the backseat.

Back in his apartment that night, Jack worked on the desert story. The Bowles anthology had just come out from Black Sparrow, bleak with scenes of Westerners misplacing trust in their Berber guides, ending up disemboweled, buried up to their necks in sand, tongueless and howling.

Jack imitated the style, a sort of white style, stony and minimal. The sentences were short. The diction was flat, lucid, impersonal as rock or dust. It was a world that had nothing, absolutely nothing human about it.

He looked out the windows. Light came up over the Drive, over the black sheath of water. This close to the river, a soft, tireless roar lifted from its cataracts, and the ticking, blinking lights from the other borough's banks became a first illuminated layer that this further whiteness—all of the Island's surging wattage —lightened like a cloud, as if the summer air were weary of its darkness and was reaching for morning. Jack thought of his newfound desert descriptions, the narrator speaking about a night and its stars as the inside lid of a pot, above and outside of which spread the blinding, limitless sheen of their god. Their god, their Allah, had always seemed to him the absence of one.

The next day he cruised the West Forties just above the Midtown line. In his rearview mirror the library lions arched their backs as he rocketed down the neglected, potholed blocks of Fifth, rustling hollow-eyed people out of dumpsters and crows up off of the crusts of restaurant food. The windows of the great safari stores shone with their gold-black ibis horns and tasseled mugs and khaki jackets.

By then, the late 70s, it was a city so on the take that the takers were getting taken. South Indian men and Russians ran out from the Port Authority with their arms in the air, waving down cabs for people, two dollars a ride. The squeegee men were there on the ramps up to the Drive. Jack paid them to back away and leave his windshield alone. Sometimes at the hack window at the end of a shift he watched the money of other drivers being counted out, a counterfeit twenty held up to the light and pushed back under the plexiglass toward the sorry driver. The man cursed in some clotted, angry Asian language, walking away toward the sinks.

The literary world was filling, too, with new charlatans. Its varied forms of failure were coming at him with new velocity, and lately he'd been talking to his friend Raifert, who told him things that would be placating only if Jack had already decided to quit writing altogether.

Raifert was in one of the big literary agencies in the Flatiron District. Big names had the chief agent—a household word in "houses" that read—negotiate with the trade giants for seven figure deals. But Raifert worked down in the "Galley", the place where English grads like himself encouraged the talentless to submit and resubmit their stuff for modest but consolidating "reading fees".

There was, of course, a significant margin the Galley had to be making in order to keep the place afloat, as the old man skimmed the lot of the half million dollar deals he was pulling in for Mailer, Gerald Ford, the big clients. Raifert and his colleagues had to get submitters to fork over more and more money for minor refreshments; no draft was ever sent to a publisher. A racket of the oldest and most basic type. The glorious anonymity of the middleman.

Jack was turned back north now, eyeing the towers of Midtown to his left. He imagined an almost visible stench from the big houses that inhabited these buildings—a rancidness like some poison gas permeating the new Republic of Letters. It was another reason he thought of giving up and heading off to the law. Thirty years before e-books, his former boss had seen the writing on the wall; small houses and their gritty, determined mid-lists were all but vanishing from the earth. Jack saw each day as a day of diminishing chances, like the number sheets dropping down in front of one another on his new, handless alarm clock. Writing becoming a new arm of the commerce hydra it had first entered the world to fight. Click. Another day down the drain. Click, click. The stats running away from him, into a widening sea, into oblivion.

At the next red light, Jack felt a growing fury with himself. His hands tightened on the wheel. Why was he just now learning what so many had already known? But it was best that it had come to him from Raifert, from an insider, a true friend. Such people came in handiest for toppling illusions, for kicking holes in your smooth innocence.

Jack had to pee and was high up on First Ave. He knew where to go. New York Hospital's ambulance bay was one of the few places that welcomed drivers on the East Side. You had to be brief and the ER couldn't be backed up. Jack also liked the old wood counters and wainscoting of the Lying-In Hospital, the country's oldest, built by British prisoners of war in the 1780s. He liked its low and even yellow light, the thickness of its incubating quiet.

When he pulled in, a dark-skinned man in some kind of foreign uniform walked toward him. When Jack turned the car off the man hustled toward the cab, breaking into a trot the last fifty feet of the incline. The man had a belt heavy with police paraphernalia, but with an odd, unfamiliar type of truncheon wagging from one of its loops.

"Your purpose here," he asked.

The man had already copied down Jack's plate number. He

backed up and checked it again and held the truncheon in front of the car, as if to block it. Jack still had the motor off.

"Bathroom," Jack said.

The officer frowned.

"Quickly," he said. Jack was surprised the man was letting him in at all. "Three minutes," he said. The man leaned against the dented fender, checking the pleats in his officer's slacks.

He lit a cigarette.

Jack was up the ramp and in the sliding doors. He saw a former philosophy professor of his, George Myro. The man was an epistemologist. They recognized each other. Jack squinted and the professor smiled, raising his chin and a pile of papers.

Their sight line was blocked immediately by a phalanx of officers: thirty, maybe fifty, in the same uniform as the man outside. But it was the plainclothesmen that flocked like birds against the glass, their black, boxy G-men suits bulked out with gun-butts and Kevlar vests. One or two would peel away and go down to the doors, check out any group of three or larger, then walk back up. They stood and moved not like law enforcement but like businessmen. Behind the dark thicket they made, the white nurses moved quickly, carrying tiny trays with cups of medications.

Jack finished and went down to the cab. The earlier soldier was gone. When he opened the door, someone shouted at him from the top of the bay. It was one of the plainclothesmen, saying something in broken English from which Jack could only extract "Excuse me." The man was up behind him in seconds. He circled the cab like the soldier had, stepped in front of it in the same way, then came back up behind Jack at the open door.

"ID," he said.

"What for?"

"I am police."

Jack turned his neck, careful to keep his movements slow.

"Let me see your badge."

The man pushed him against the glass of the driver's window. He pressed his body against Jack's, his great chest, the hard steel of the machine pistol in the shoulder holster digging into Jack's back. The man's breath smelled like mint, cardamom. Jack wanted to cry out for help but something stopped him, a feeling halfway down his chest, knotting and warming—a fat, hottening ball.

Another voice was coming down the ramp, yelling, an American and a New York accent.

"What the fuck?" the new man said. "Get away from him."

Out of the corner of his eye, Jack saw the tattered jacket of a New York police officer. Just the dark blue uniform, the chest and belt full of improbably heavy devices. Patrol beat. Nothing fancy. He pulled the plainclothesman off Jack and turned him around, pushing him down to a seat on the fender. The folded, steel stock of the tech pistol stuck up from under the foreigner's armpit. The cop kept pushing him, forcing him down, spreading and flattening the man's arms and staying away from the weapon.

He held his finger against the agent's sweating nose. "Get the fuck outa here," he said, his left hand on the butt of his revolver.

The man stared at him, inches away from his face. He brushed himself off, took a couple of deep breaths, still staring. He looked up toward the bay desks, the stands of luggage. A long row of his ravenish colleagues, arms crossed, stood watching everything, pulling cigarettes in and out of their mouths.

The agent put his head down and started walking up toward them.

"You alright?" the cop asked Jack.

Jack opened his door and sat down and looked up at him.

"Yeah. Thanks."

"No problem," the cop said, his Queens accent strong, welcome as a breeze in the face to Jack. "These little Persian fuckers are throwing their weight around. It's gonna be their funeral if this shit keeps up."

Jack remembered the Persian grad students at Berkeley. All were activists, dreading and hiding from the Shah's Savak agents, putting newspapers in front of their faces on the surveilled marches. Jack's cousin at Texas said Savak had kidnapped students, renditioned them to sites in Canada; people had simply disappeared out of her engineering classes in Austin.

"What's going on?" Jack asked. "Who's in there?"

The officer's radio crackled when he opened his mouth to answer. "89 Copy," he said into the mike.

"Who's here?"

"89 you good?" asked the voice.

"89 affirmative. Bullies on the block."

"The big man, that's who. The big-ass, square head, big man."

Jack angled his head into a question.

"The one who sits," the officer said, nodding down at Jack's paper on the dash. "The one who sits on the Peacock Throne."

Jack thanked him again and started the car. He coasted down the cobbled horseshoe and pulled back into the shade of First.

He looked down toward Queensborough Bridge in his rearview. He remembered a photo of his grandfather that his maternal grandmother pulled out of a biscuit tin once and held up to him. The skinny man, in suspenders and with his Roosevelt cigarette holder, was leaning against his long-haul truck, parked there under the bridge in its changeless 30s sameness. He'd started as a farmer. Then he'd taken up trucking and eventually, moving from upriver Pittsburgh, went to tire building in the various Akron factories. He moved from there to sales, and finally, in the last years before he died, to a low-level management job. The ladder of ripening richness had risen, blue collar to white, one trembling, downward-looking step at a time.

The locusts and elms of the street's east side, the clouds of their branches, were bending in a sudden wind, their heaving weight of leaves hung close, flung loose like spinning coins. They clattered on Jack's windshield in tiny taps, fat clumps, until he had to turn on his wipers to see the waving hand of a far-off fare.

That night in a dream the leaves blew forward into the open culvert of his skull, whirling against its sides, spitting and sliding, gathering into a sort of frozen winding stair at its center and then ever so gracefully loosening, bending, spinning in green and yellow and browning flakes through the black of his closed eyes. Then they were gone. He saw and heard nothing but his deep and even breathing.

In the morning when he sat up in bed he knew he would stay. He would write. He would write on his Harrod's black cabman's pad at red lights and at stands, and if he got a long string of reds on Park Avenue would pull over and creak up the parking brake, listening, as he did at the hospital, to the Checker's idle under his barely more audible scratching.

He would give it another year, maybe another two or three. He would put his pages—what a weighty thing a page was!—out into the world and wait for it to be thrown back at him, worked on and then sent out again, returned and worked on again, turned backward and forward in the paper's idling, waiting space.

He looked at the clock. He was late and Reznick would dock him, he knew, by a fare and a half. When he got out of the shower the TV was on. Phil Donahue was talking to feminists sitting in tall chairs. Then he walked down through the audience with his mic, taking questions, the picture of earnestness.

The screen went dark and there was a beep, a special bulletin.

A grainy video from far away showed lines of people forming, moving uneasily underneath the seal of what was obviously some government building, an embassy. They were blindfolded. Students surrounded them, wagging their fingers and punching the dusty air with their fists.

The Farmer Wears The Crown of Thorns

If you wish to supplant someone, to substitute yourself for them, could wishes be like wavelets, partial causes, small curling waters like the rivers Roger fished flowing north to Erie, the inland sea that could create or be created from anything—glaciers, ice-swales, beginnings and endings of ages before men walked these grassy places, the flattened green.

What was the difference between the great and final cause and its tributaries? Roger wondered this in the months before what happened to Hazen, the one who had risen in old man Jay's eyes as the splendid issue, who had shed his clumsiness and was now the planner, the craftsman, the farm's bright star in the shadowed, cropless valley pushing up against Ohio.

He thought of how much he hated his brother's name, his loose white shirt that bobbed now on the tractor seat, working the gears that clanged like an anchor chain, a compass needle finding the family's new direction—north or true north it mattered not, pulling all of them now up through the weirs and harrows.

Hazen the rising one, Roger one to be risen above. No two could be equal in bringing up things of the earth, turning great beasts into fountains of meat and milk and the leather that wallets were made out of.

Hazen looked back at him and smiled. Roger did not smile back.

Each of them saw the farm as their legacy, their destiny.

Roger was prudent, some would say conservative. Hazen was all progress, taking on risk as a sort of necessary breath. The wobble and blur of their debates took over dinners, holiday suppers.

Hazen passed the bowl of peas under his mother's nose before she had even finished grace. Matie grabbed the bowl and placed it over in front of Roger.

"What's the bank want for the loan? The milking machines?"

Hazen didn't seem up for talking.

"I'll ask again tomorrow. Our broker is good people."

"Ballpark?" Roger asked, dishing himself a pile of green he'd turn into a pyramid when he was little.

"Hundred thousand on the land. Straight collateral."

Roger was going to fake one of his chocking sounds. But he wanted to give Jay and Matie a break.

The father said nothing. The old man could hardly hear.

* * *

The following day was blueprint day, what they called Fridays now. Their cousin Liza was an accountant. She kept the books. Roger thought she was partial to Hazen, but then at times thought he was imagining it all. When she leaned now to put the sand-filled weights on the prints he looked down the front of her blouse. She looked back sharply at him once. But today she was in a hurry, all business, all taps and totals on her pocket calculator. Her aloofness around him was puzzling, because he was also a man for figures, rows and columns of them stuck crookedly into machines and then spitting up out of them like new clean snow. He tried to figure her snobbery out, for years, for endless ways of thought. But she pushed him away, turned up her nose at Roger's wife Vanessa, kept them out of the charmed circle she and Hazen would guard like sentinels.

Liza spread the blueprints, smoothed them with her whitened nails which seemed as white as the lines that floated up from the unrolled sheets. Roger loved the blueprints that pictured plankings and peaks for unbuilt barns, for switches and panels and hoses that ended in glass udder tubes, where before there had been hands, squeezing and pulling for a hundred years.

He didn't expect them to take his advice, take what he'd say into the whole of the magical process. He just wanted to be listened to. To be considered. Attention must be paid, like the playwright said.

He leaned forward as Hazen's hand traced the lines out of the consoles and across the floors. It was a mighty architecture. Few people of their ilk had entered the world of milking machines. The hands on the udders, the stools would be things for a reliquary. When he saw the calloused fists of their own hired men now he saw the bones beneath the skin, the sticklike squeaking of human hinges. He gazed across the blue-white grid. It was the future. It was a picture of the future.

Liza spent a lot of time on a set of tall books, back against the office wall which only she seemed to have the key to. Hazen was hypnotized by the blueprints, and when Roger moved forward to watch Hazen looking at them, Liza interposed herself between them, twirling the ring of keys smartly around her index finger.

"Vanessa, how is she?"

"O, good," said Roger. "Thank you for asking."

Liza seemed to like Vanessa more than Roger, and Roger sometimes thought of this as progress, and other times a kind of double insult.

"What's back there?" Roger asked, nodding to the desk where the books were.

"A load of crap," Liza answered. "More manure than you'd see in the grazing vale." She smiled, then all three of them grinned. The blueprints always did this, reduced them to their common purpose. It was like a fire which they gathered around, a substitute hearth. Liza rolled them up and Hazen had sets of rubber bands for each end.

"Stay for supper?" Roger asked her.

"A pleasure, a pure pleasure. Always is."

* * *

The hired men, now three of them, ate at the table with the family. Matie had only one requirement. The men had to wear shirts. Shirts with collars that hadn't been worn outside. Domer had a brother, Wade, and Wade's son Earl, with a bodybuilder's biceps, was indispensable for the haying and binding. "Big guns on him," Jay said once. Matie winced at the comparison. She had been raised Quaker. Guns were the Other, made for things all humanity should be moving away from. Hazen reminded her that the farm had been given to her own father by the new Union his soldiery had preserved.

Dishes were passed around with a nimble elegance that covered the black energy flowing between the brothers. Hazen watched Vanessa dab her mouth with a Kleenex. The hired men ate like savages, men who hadn't seen a plate of food for weeks.

Roger saw Hazen looking at Vanessa, as he often did. Hazen had never married. "Too much treasure out there to dig," he'd say. "Too much in the trees to shake loose. A wife and kids would ruin all adventures."

Roger knew Hazen admired his wife's great beauty, the fierceness of her poise, the body of a sylph that would never leave her.

Roger squinted at his brother's gaze, and Hazen looked up at their father. Jay of the last century, of the sleeve holders and suspenders. The old man took extra shots of the port whose quality he derided, calling it the brandy of the damned.

The women did the dishes and gossiped. The men sat in recliners and talked about football, Civil War battles. Jay nodded off while Roger fidgeted, seeing Hazen go into the kitchen, feigning conversation while he surveyed what was Roger's better self, his only prize.

Roger said he was going outside to check the well pumps. In the workroom he went to the back where Liza had put the long ledger books and pulled them out. One had clean balance sheets with no markings. The other said, at the top, "Not For Auditors." It had larger amounts all bracketed with penciled numbers and column titles. Roger had always wanted in on the firm's finances, wishing the accounts to be farm documents and transparent with their profit accrual corpuses. But Liza was the designated steward. The right book's extra funds had gone somewhere, but Roger, and he knew his parents, had no idea where. When he was closing the cover a staple cut his thumb. He wiped away the blood drops and then spit on his handkerchief and watered it clear in little circles.

The day it happened was a bright, cold day. Shadows of clouds blew over the sheep sorrel, whirling above it like a twisting cape. The pasture grass shimmered, the trees shone emerald over the fences where the grasses ended.

Hazen was on the John Deere, Wade riding on the metal running board. They were heading to the churning shed to fix a leak. One of the mistakes they made was putting the tools in their belts—there was plenty of room in the toolbox behind the seat. There was a giant pond of mud in a dip in the grass path. Hazen drove forward into it, guessing it was a foot high max. He entered fast, hoping to splash through. But the tractor immediately started to sink. The mud went up to the top of the tractor's wheels. Wade's jumper went black up to his knees, and he held fast to the tractor's engine block and started to laugh at first.

The tractor sank quickly, very quickly. Roger watched—Jay had told him about these sinkholes, coming after heavy rains. He ran to the garage and grabbed a pole, ten or twelve feet long, with a wishbone prong stretching out from a yellow trunk that had been painted, sanded by one of the hands who was good with finish work.

By the time Roger got down to the sinkhole's rim, the tractor was plunging at an unreal speed, like grass fires he'd seen spreading in the straw. He couldn't see Wade at all and figured he had jumped free somehow. The mud was up under Hazen's arms.

When the redness of panic had drained from his face, his skin whitened with a more sharpened, practical fear. He looked back and forward in quick snaps, conveying a gratitude that his brother was doing all he could. He leaned right and pointed at the bubbles of Wade's air under the surface.

But Roger wasn't doing all he could. His grip was only halfway up the wishbone struts. He could have given its reach another ten or twelve inches by grabbing the last segments of the prongs. But he didn't. Someone watching from above or at a distance would be as fooled as Hazen. But someone by the pool would be able to see the abbreviation of Roger's efforts. The calculated gesture. The holding back.

What lay above the line was Hazen's blood and gulps of

oxygen. What lay below were generations of ambitious dairymen who had moved too fast. They were the drowned and the saved of the afterlife, traversing halls whose ceiling was this black muck where the sun flung spangles, brightening, wavering coins.

Roger heard the sirens of the fire trucks, and when the long one backed down into the swale, a yellow ladder swung out and Hazen, his shoulders covered, reached up and grabbed it.

"Harness, harness!" a fireman yelled, and Hazen threw the canvas vest around himself, wiping his hands on the tightening burlap. But the ladder twisted him, snapped him around in one direction, then jerked him in the other. The coat of mud slipped off of him and with each ladder jerk what was left went off in blackened spray.

That is when everyone heard it, the snap of his vertebrae. He had gotten what, in the old days before the electric chair in Harrisburg, was called the perfect hangman's fracture. His useless limbs would stay that way.

They fished Wade's body out with an angling gaffer. The firemen put Hazen on a stretcher under a mound of blankets and jackets. Liza wasn't there to run to him. Vanessa was, and she gave Roger a menacing look, motioning him over with an irritated sweep of her hand.

When they stood in the hospital room in Pittsburgh, somebody said that Liza was on her way. Roger watched the doctor's hands rove over the X-ray mounted and lit from behind. He pointed out the broken trail of the spine, the free-floating triangles of bone. The x-rays had an azure cast, and the doctor's hands, feminine and small, reminded him of Liza tracing the white lines along the blueprints.

When Hazen was out of anesthesia he looked up at Roger, standing beside his bed, and thanked him: *thank you boss, thank you brother. I never should have gone through that patch.*

Roger patted Hazen's sheets, looked at his watch, and went into the bathroom and vomited.

It was a slow, sometimes violent job of erasing the events from his memory. There were splinters of guilt he pulled loose from the doors behind doors that led to the horror of it, the surfaces smoothed flat by the wood plane of forgetting. It was like whitewash on the sides of a new spring barn. But inside of him each room of thought was lightless, and when he left its darkness and opened another door, it got darker.

Roger had to carry on, but the work of erasure was exhausting and nauseating. He was the man of the place, and the endless ways of thought had to give way to new tasks and efficiencies, small lamps flickering in emptiness.

* * *

Wade's funeral was four days later. His immense wife suspended from her wide black dress a gaggle of stunned children.

The widow was seated in a sort of apex the misarrangement of the chairs had made. The minister was dreadful, and Wade had been in Vietnam and the head of the burial detail brought the triangled flag to her, kneeling on an aging knee and saluting.

But just after this, under the fiddles and Irish drum of a Bluegrass hymn his friends had written decades before, Liza sat by Hazen's wheelchair, a kind of almost-widow, and looked over at Vanessa and Roger. Under her unbuttoned coat, hidden from the gun-hating Matie, she bunched her fist into a makeshift pistol stock. She raised its invisible barrel toward Roger and Vanessa, and when Liza saw that he saw her, her eyes narrowed, and a barely detectable grin grew on her face so that the edges of her mouth twisted like a crooked pin.

Then she raised her thin pink index finger and pulled the trigger, faster and then even faster, two shots for Roger and two shots for V.

Summer's Blood

I.

To make one was to make a face, really, a human face—eyes, nose, mouth and teeth—and to carve it up out of earth, or something part of it, that grew up out of it, something like dust—like God made up Adam out of dead dirt and breath. It was to have your parents let you do something complicated, as complicated as the things they did, or God did every day, just this one day. They let you use a knife, they let you cut. They gave you the power to make something like a life. But when you pushed through the skin you knew it was death, too, that had been put in your hands.

At Christmas you didn't make anything, at Thanksgiving nothing. And nothing at Easter that was fun for a boy, the dyed eggs smooth and hot and amazing the way their whiteness took the color, but really a frilly thing, something for girls to do. Nothing at anything else, either. Only here, only now, could you take something up and carve out a head and put a candle in behind the eyes to make a soul, a mind, a Geist as Mrs. Bernsteiner would say. (Geist was something a knife should usually go through, but here was a time when you made it with one, like a wand, waving hard shapes out of next to nothing.) It wasn't a holiday like any of the others, but it was the one of making—building up something, this thing, out of fire and dirt and—what was it?—fruit?

The best place to get them wasn't a farm but just a house, Slayton's, sitting in the woods on old Hanley Road. The drive took you through four covered bridges, over the Clear and Black Fork rivers, past the fruit farm which you floated by slowly. It was fall, and the Keenans who ran it served free cider, their eight whooping kids running down the lawn from E.B's mansion to grab the white cone cups from a stack, knocking the tap, the brown blood sputtering, going over the cup's lip, colder as its color cleared. Down from there, that highest of the county's tiny mountains, you came to a darkened glade of moss and rot still leopard-spotted with what the sun let down—like the deep water light you saw on TV laying on sunken boats, on chests of treasure. That was where you found Slayton's, just barely.

It needed, you thought, a farm stuck to it. A barn or a shed. At least some outbuildings. At first it looked square and serious as a farmhouse, with uncurtained windows like worried eyes. But it didn't have the whiteness, the feeling of warmth. You imagined lights inside a farmhouse. Their place was grey—cave-cold with hickory shade. Its siding was dark as a charcoal mare's.

Nobody could figure the Slaytons out. Some say it was the Old Mother who kept it that way. Others blamed her son; the lazier he got the darker it grew. His lupus wife couldn't do anything either, her steel crutches inching up at you when you drove in. Walked like a spider, my father said. Nobody knew where Mother's husband went.

They themselves looked just like the place, like they could have come out of one of its walls. When you visited you wanted to get back to the patch. But they always took you through, as if that was the payment, before letting you pick for your dime or quarter. Blanche pointed with a crutch to where you should park. The half-off door swung back at your face.

You wanted to go in but then you didn't. But the swing of the door made you know you would. Mr. Carter, in Sunday School, talked about that feeling. "Dread," he called it. Drawn to it, drawn away. We wondered enough to go in but then stopped: at the sound of the clink, the lock falling behind us. (Grandma Jana said Grandpa spoke in the bed as he died in a soft falling sound like that, almost sweet and musical, in the great space he entered. He didn't seem scared. Maybe inside were the same stamping cattle, the milk cans he held every morning of life.)

Which all seemed right, this idea of a door. The spirits' doors opened on this one night. The dead came through them to dance unseen, to be with we living, who hadn't been called yet.

But that came later, thinking about that. What hit you when you first stood in the room was the heat, the warm block of it coming down around you like a coat. October wasn't that cold but they kept the furnace on. The coal pan was bad. The chunks of it slipped in the fire, bleeding and deepening in the flames. Soot blew through the registers and blackened the dust. Rude people, my mother said, wrote their names in it on the tops of things.

A morning's worth was on their faces by the time you saw them there. Mr. wore it thickest, like a five o'clock shadow. He never ignored you. "Golf ball eyes," was what Bub called him. Bub said he wore a diaper Doctor Reed fixed him up with. I looked for pins under his Oshkosh but his hands were always there, quick and busy with picking, bringing up seeds he pushed into his gums. He used a wheelchair a lot; my mother said polio. Bub had heard nothing was wrong with him: "The coot just likes to sit," he said. Dennis Anderkin's Mom told him the same. He'd given up on the world, May said—no point in walking through it anymore. "Malingerer," was my father's opinion, the longest word I ever heard him use.

My Grandmother Jana said he did every foul and unnatural thing a human could commit. He picked the scabs that grew from his hopeless fence mending and hedge trimming. The cracks of his skin were filled with dirt, his nails all black purple and soft bone whiteness. Jana said this by itself could send you to the hospital. But Mr. even picked the hairs of his nose. This would instantly kill most people. She told us about a man in the Bible who'd been set up for hundreds of years of life, picked one hair and dropped dead like a bird.

The old mother would sit in a wheelchair too when she got tired of wandering and swatting the curtains. The swatting and cobbing drained her of blood. She slid down in the chair, her skin white as the curtains the window's breeze wrapped her in.

Mrs. minded the kitchen, the patches, the "business," running in from somewhere always out of sight. On this trip I came right up on her, leaving my father and the girls in front. Lila Slayton had been smart, maybe still was—a physics degree from Brown, a shelf of the Great Books. But her hair was wild as cabbage grass, her teeth stained brown like a man's who chewed. She jumped when I came up behind her at the sink. Her hands held globs of rags she'd been soaking.

"Jacky," she said. "Come for your pumpkin? How's your Grandmother Jana?"

"Ma'am," I said, "she's fine."

"Come for your pumpkin?" She came up to me, closer. I could smell the Southern Comfort on her breath. I saw once the two pint bottles she kept behind the orange juice jug on the icebox shelf. I wasn't snooping, just looking for water. Its label was the thing I loved: the etching of a paddle steamer like my other Grandma Ada and her sisters—all the Willcoxans— had ridden down the Ohio on to Gallipolis. Smoke floated out of the boat stacks on the label, over high-hatted people waving from the banks.

"Yes," I said. "Like usual."

"Like usual," she said, looking down at my shoes, new bright sneakers like nothing she'd seen before, never going—I knew—to stores where they'd be. She squinted at them, then gave a sad nod, the nod of a railroad bum or a full-on madman like Speedy Heiser. Then she looked away and into the sink, drying her hands to come out back.

The door the garden opened into made no sound. It was like a wall of dark air itself, hingeless and smooth with nothing to its touch but the slightest cool sense of passage. It opened out. It told you the step was down, into something darker. This was the place where the patches started.

I followed her, walking as slow as I could in the dusk. She lifted the leaves with the end of her ashplant. Little clouds of dust came up. The first ones we saw still had a good color. The long months of sun had poured down their orange.

"Jacky." I turned around. My father stood in the doorway. Elly's pixie bangs were there under his hand, wet from running.

"Why George," Mrs. said, straightening up. "Come down here and pick out something."

Both came down the steps, Elly uneasily, him shifting her over the last cracked one. She swung like a puppet on his long, bare arm.

"How's your mother, George?"

"Oh fine, fine," he said. His eyes were down under the leaves and I could tell he wasn't listening. It was like walking with him when he hunted. Everything else disappeared to him. There were only his eyes and the thing he waited for—the thing which was everywhere and nowhere at once.

I went on ahead. A cat jumped up. They were everywhere at Slayton's, circling the furniture, nosing in cupboards, laying on the Old Mother's doll-lined shelves. This was a calico. Orange and black, it looked right for the pumpkins

I kept going, kicking, watching for the perfect one. The sky was clear, and the space it became seemed far from us. Bright roads of stars waved up out of the buttonwoods. The breeze coming through them chilled my skin, and somehow made me think of cutting again—the cutting that sent things from world to world. The road between heaven and earth was a blade. It let you in and it let you out. It let you pass over like the dancing Geists. I thought of the movies of babies being born—the cord had to break before they were here. And it let you out.

"There," she said behind me. This one was big, but not too big. It hadn't grown enough to sag and flatten. The cloud of its dust hung there in the floodlight. She held the leaves when my foot pulled away.

"Right there," she said.

"Where'd you get your pumpkin?" Leo asked.

We were in the treehouse of the Grand Kazan. He headed the house and owned it and set the rules during his reign. They never changed much because nobody could ever think of anything new. Just the basics: no girls, no parents, no kids older than the GK. He watched over the footlocker that held the things we stood for: wampum belts and arrowheads, books about screwing (*Sexology* was one that Tim got from his mother's attic, by Dr. Albert Ellis), and the still-beating Poe hearts we'd get someday from other kids, from other clubs, kids we'd kill and cut up and tear the skin off in strips like the Iroquois did in battle. We'd vowed to be like them, without pity and vengeful for our fallen.

Rolf Bernsteiner was the GK now. We all had German names—Hartmann, Wolff—sounds tongue-rolling tough: Gevertz and Fasnacht and Werner (my own). The kids from clubs that called us Huns were German too, so that didn't make much sense. Besides, we were Indians, and whoever had to learn it would learn it at the stake.

"Slaytons," I said. I put my green apple branch—my offering, my talisman—in the center of the circle we made with our chairs.

"Weird bunch," said Roxy Falde. "Like a bunch of frigging trolls."

"Like the dwarfs," Tim said, "at Disneyland. But with no stocking caps." He liked knowing that we'd never seen Disneyland. His dad was rich, did something with satellites. They flew to California every summer.

"The dolls the old lady has give me the creep-o's," Bub said. He put the bottom of his palms against his lips and made a farting sound.

"Ditto," said Roxy, "wrapped up like that."

"She collects them," I said. "She's crippled." Bub's sound kept up, trailed off. "Gives her something to do."

"But when you go in! Gadzooks," Bub said. "It's like something in hell. Dead people on shelves. It's like bleachers full of stiffs."

"In cellophane," said Tim.

"Saran wrap," said Rolf.

"Keeps off the dust," I said, and pictured the rows of them, twisted and frozen. This last time I hadn't paid them much attention. But there they were each visit, built and set there, it seemed, with no thought or feeling—just a constant, silent, mindless attention. They were like the crowd that waited in front of you at Sunday School recital or scout camp when you had to make a speech and had nothing to say. Awful little hollow people waiting for something, something you'd promised to give them, only you, but found that you couldn't. They weren't like the pumpkins—raw and waiting for life. They'd already had a part of it and wanted more, all their eyes watching your little evasions.

"I saw Vick Schechter's baloobas," volunteered Leo.

"Oh futz you did," said Zimmerman.

"Did."

"Did not."

"Where at?"

"Right here," Leo said, pounding his chest with gorilla beats. "Two," he said. "They look alike."

"Where *at*?" asked Zimmerman again. His forehead was red. This was serious business.

"Up against the window of their bathroom."

I thought of how this might have been possible. The Rieffs lived next door to the Schechters, in those clapboard houses that lined Maple Street and that you'd see once in a while coming down West Main on a flatbed truck. Leo's bedroom window looked straight across to her bath, and I let the picture of it clear into something believable—the rising steam, pink flashes through the frosted panes.

All of it irked me, his thinking about it. My hunger for her had begun. She deserved my thoughts, only mine to belong to. She had just turned sixteen, ripe and lovely. None of us, really, could stop thinking about her. She was my babysitter, Walt and Libby Schechter's daughter. She had the street whirling in the smell of new sex. She had my father's young eye, but my mother forgave it. Vick's mother Lib was my mother's best friend, partly because of her being a nurse, that circle of women who had flown from the trap of husband and house and out into the secret night world of Marshfield General's sneakered halls— white doves of freedom, they must have seemed to her. She'd talk to Lib on the phone for hours, sighing after an episode of Ben Casey. Lib would go on about working the OR, in the soupy red sea of a real doctor's hooks and clamps and trays of bright knives.

"The closest anyone's gotten to them," I said, hating myself for it, but feeling the claim of her stronger than anything else I could say, "was me and Bub. Bug collecting."

It was true. We got them for her biology class: everythingwe could find from Ridey's field —Viceroys and dragonflies and luna moths; blind, burrowing beetles with heads and eyes like clots of blood. We took turns standing on the top stair of her porch while she kneeled to pin them, lifting them gently from each jar. Her breasts were golden and freckled, nested loosely in her soft sling bras. I wanted to press my face against her, nose their rubbery tips, touch paradise. I had some vague knowledge it would transfigure me, give some answer to any question my life could ever ask. She squealed when she drove the pins through, and watching her made small pains flick up in my chest, as if matches were being lit there.

"I saw them. Her," said Leo again, pushing his glasses up on his nose. "I saw her from the front and side when she was drying. And from the back. She spread the towel across the rod." We saw it, all of us, the legs widening, the cleft of hair between from the back. I grew redder, and knew they could see the color coming into me.

"Did you see her pajoda?" asked Sowash.

Leo made dog sounds, nodding his head up and down to sniff.

"Was it fuzzy, like a beaver?" he asked.

Leo caught it all in the same long nod.

I was furious now. I knew I would stutter if I tried to talk. A secret had been torn from me, a thing of my own imagining taken without permission. I wanted to choke Leo, to get him down and put a stick across his throat and push each end down with my knees. But like all the rest of them, Leo was bigger than me. He could have choked me without a stick.

"Did everybody go to Slaytons?" I asked.

"Does the Pope shit in the woods?" said Sowash. I liked Sowash. There was something adventurous and military about his family. His father was a colonel who owned a truck and a printing press.

"Only place to get your pump," said Leo. "Now all we got to do is pump it." I felt better now, getting her out of their talk at least.

"We've got a big one," Jim Roper said. His last school picture had a fly sitting on top of his crewcut, and he'd told me once, in a soft voice full of shame, that his parents were planning to divorce—unheard of then except in the movie magazines.

We all were growing tired now. Some of us crawled out to the ironing boards we nailed between the forks of the larger branches. They were bowed by the rain and smoothed of chips and splinters enough to be easy on our backs, and made a good, almost level porch for the place, a good place to lay down and watch the stars.

I saw Cassiopeia, the Queen. The legs of her chair were like columns of diamonds. I thought of being in love with Vick, of what the look of love from her would be like—smiling and flushed and thrilled to come close, seeing me when my parents left not as a parent but as a woman, wanting me, wanting to give herself over. And that feeling grew to the strongest and sweetest of waking dreams —that something lay waiting for me to find it, something of the strongest and loveliest power.

II.

Then it was finally carving time, the night we all headed over to Reeds. Mr. Reed had the family living in the basement while he finished the house. Its floors were full of wood shavings and steel rods and lumber, so the parents voted their place the place. Bub called old man Reed "The Fly", and Roger Jessup called him "eccentric," a word I never got a good hold on. But there had to have been something to it, the way Ralph yelled out his words, as if you couldn't hear him even when you were close. He bought threshing machines at back country auctions, and ran them for no reason on weekend mornings. But then I thought how everyone could be eccentric to somebody else, how my father called Roger that because he held his gun funny. So maybe it was one of those words that meant everything, everything and nothing. One that you used in place of understanding.

Mr. Reed worked nights at Ideal Electric. He was a lead man who pulled parts down from one belt and made them into big-dialed radios on another—the ones whose grills and knobs looked like a face. (My father kept one on the toolbench shelf, the dial's soft light spreading across the jars of screws and two-penny nails that stretched our reflections when we passed by the table saw.) Mrs. Reed led the cub scout troop. My mother claimed she tried to turn them Pentecostal, speaking in tongues at their Weblos fire.

She spread us out Indian style in the unfinished upstairs. We put our pumpkins between our legs, and walked up to the table to pick our instrument. It was scattered with things from Mr. Reed's toolbox—files and pliers, all glimmering with oil. It had a sliding lid, and when Mrs. wasn't watching I opened it, closed and opened it again. It gave off a smell of iron and kerosene.

We never cut ourselves, and I think one of the reasons the mothers let Martha host us was that she had watched boys before, guarded them against their carelessness, one of "all God's dangers" she always talked about. This time I chose a buck knife like the one my uncle Yeager used to skin the deers my father shot. I walked back to the wall with it, feeling its weight, running my thumb up against the knobbed horn where the blade started.

I started my lid with square cuts, pulling till the juice came up through the crack. I wanted an octagon, a hexagon, whatever it would be. Most cut in circles and didn't get far. Everybody eventually all got going, the same sawing sound—like a thumbnail grating on coil wire. My stem was still on, long and curled and furry: like what's left of the cord once the baby is out.

My lid, I thought, was a piece of geometry. Brought up into something from paper and thought. Inside was mush and soft seed and plant blood. It was much, much brighter than the skin: the thick blood all brains floated in, surrounding and feeding it, pouring in life. I wondered what would happen if you cooked it. People ate the brains of cows. It made Liz Taylor faint in "Giant."

The mush closed fast and cold as water around my fingers. Its color mixed under the white of my nails. It was too light to stain though, a melon's soft color, one mostly water, with a water's clearness. I pulled it out with a coffee mug and scraped the meat from the walls. I turned it upside down and knocked. Even that wet, every seed fell out.

I made the mouth with lots of teeth, not most of them missing like most people did. I left a few of the bottoms out, and made a good square cut for the one missing top. It would be more real that way, like Speedy Hiser's or the bums that cooked at the depot fires and smiled up at your car when you slowed for the tracks. The eyes were the hardest. They could be anything—squares or circles or the triangles everybody made. But the knife seemed to fall into a shape of its own, nothing more than a normal eye. I leaned the whole thing up on my knees and pushed the carved parts in with the knifetip.

Now it was time to really get going, to give it its brain, its final light. Mrs. had come around a lot earlier to watch. She hadn't said anything when she passed mine. I guessed it was alright with her, but it wouldn't have bothered me if it hadn't been. I liked herand Bob in a way and felt sorry for Mr.—his whole life a mess of sad, scattered trinkets—but I had enough of my father's contempt for them in me, enough to feel that where they were wasn't where you should end up. I knew that I couldn't, that I wouldn't end up there. And I also knew—far, far more importantly—that my father wasn't as sure of that as me.

She was behind me now, holding a box of candles spiraled and tipped like a bullet, the color of dirty, mud-made ice. I trimmed the wick and lit it with one of the long blue tip matches she laid in front of us. It leaned well going in. No wax went down the side. I rested it on the lid edge while its bottom filled with the clear, hot drops, and stood its end in the center of that.

Mrs. came around a third time, smiling a little with her little mouse face. I put on the top, put it on the floor, pushed it toward the center with my stocking feet.

"Well," she said, smiling more, "There now. There."

I was really too old to trick or treat, so when that night came I talked my mother into letting me go out with the Legacy brothers. They promised to drive the Nova—silver, from their father's lot. I let Elly light the pumpkin before the first beggars came. My mother lit a small pink birthday candle and put it in Elly's hand, and lifted her over it so she could touch the wicks. When the big candle flared their faces blazed. My mother said "Good," and Elly squealed. We put it on the milkbox and turned the welcome mat sideways. The flame threw its color down onto the rubber. When Legacy took us out East Main in fourth and made the cross and upward kick to fifth we flew back in our seats, and finally felt free then, part of the night, like ghosts going out over the ground. The breeze in our hair made us feel like pure thought, or fire or air and no earthly thing.

One by one we saw signs of magic. Mrs. Wyrzynski had hung her Indian corn to ward off evil spirits. My uncle worked with her husband Detlef. His coverall pockets were filled with amulets. She thought there were spirits in the place they worked—a roundhouse of darkness and crumbling brick, where hammers rang like bells in front of glowing forges and splashed fireballs of iron onto the ground. She'd given Detlef a thumb-sized stone, face-shaped and smoothed by a river in Lodz, where Germans—like you, she said to us once—shot three of her brothers in front of her eyes. She never had a jack-o'-lantern, only this corn. She'd told us of Poland, of Lithuania, where Halloween was called All Hallow's Eve. The dead came across the rivers and roads of heaven, the Himmelfahrstrassen, just to watch you all night, remembering life. Legacy said old Wodja was crazy.

"She's off her nut," he said, peeling rubber in front of her walk.

"A basketball," said Leo.

But the rest of us wanted to take what she'd told us, throw it into the pot and keep it. Magic was magic and old people knew. They came from places where miracles happened. Fire crawled on the ponds at night. Hourglass sand ran from bottom to top. Streets filled with crocodiles in the middle of winter. "In goddamn Poland," Bub said, in a vote for belief. The old ones knew. They knew and had seen or they knew who had seen. You couldn't laugh off voices with a ring like hers. It was the sound of what had happened.

And it rose, that magic, each street you went down, like the rising peeps of morning birds. The kids in costumes all held hands—bag-headed, draped with sheets or crepe, the girls in pointed witch hats like giant thorns or soft white good witch angel dresses, with wands that ended in sprinkled stars. Some wore the plastic store-bought Dracula and Frankenstein masks, with PJ bottoms the kids burned up in, Bub said, like marshmallows for being dumbo futzes. "The really sad thing is the candy melted."

We stopped at the corner of Fredrick and Clever. It was the longest chain of hands we saw. A pretty girl led them, as pretty as Vick and probably a babysitter. When I looked closer she seemed to have a uniform, something a beauty parlor lady or nurse would wear. Their masks floated strangely over their bags, cocked in different directions, and they turned around each other like they were dizzy. When we got close enough I saw they didn't have masks. Their eyes were wide apart and rolled to each side. Their faces looked squeezed. They all had bangs. They looked down at their shoes, like blind people walking.

"'Tards," said Leo.

I knew they were from the Shriner's home. Their faces got wide in our lights and they smiled. They moved so slowly, just holding on, as if to move at all were pain.

None of us said anything for a while. We passed the Junior High, then Church Street and the Square. The light was green—I saw it the same time Legacy did—and he punched it hard, knowing the only cops would be behind us now, out of hearing in the parking lot behind the gym.

Going down Plymouth felt like the first long falling ride on the Blue Streak up at Cedar Point. He made it this way by tearing us through and coasting the hill so our stomachs flipped. We forgot what we'd seen, or added it to the long night's strangenesses. Some strangeness, some magic would always be sad. Some of it showed the mistakes of the world. The knife could slip. The candle could drop. Anything could do it, and it was best not to think about.

Legacy punched it. I was scared of a crash. I put my knees up under my chin. My hair flattened over my cold, tight ears. The air was wet and full of fog. The trees and lawns made their morning dew. The dark air seemed meant to hold more than itself—everything rising to a sign of something. We felt the night around us as restless, but with a restlessness we had spun ourselves. We felt our whole past lives flying by, like men on a ship watching land disappear. There was nothing behind us we felt like remembering. This moment would always be only this moment.

Down the long slide of Plymouth and Smith, and out past the mill shanties all of us saw them: the pumpkins and porches or big rocks they sat on, the stream of them melded together by something. We had made ours and someone made these. But someone or something had made us up, at least into whatever filled us then. All of it—candles and bushes, ourselves—was a long, rich thought that the night had grown.

The eyes and mouths and sometimes lidless points of flame went on and on and on like a river, one that the moon had shattered in pieces. The town was gone once we crossed the tracks. The country houses jumped out from their trees. Legacy gunned it. The faces flew faster—miles of whirling and grinning fire.

White Prairie

There's a sucker born every minute. When we were growing up my father was still a salesman, and felt he knew the truth of this adage better than anyone. He felt it was especially true of the vacationing American family, so when summer came around he spoke more often of the terrible dangers of innocence. He was convinced the interstates were lined with vipers mounted at cash registers, modern highwaymen laying in wait for Norman Rockwell's stationwagonfull of happy, red-cheeked hayseeds. He knew all they needed was the slip of the foot that would make him one of the vast unmonied, one of the fleeced—one of the sad people old P.T. had seen coming.

We always began these journeys in the middle of the night. The idea was to get as far as we could before sunrise and the heat it brought up on the flatlands. We rose and washed like silent animals, searching for things we might have forgotten by the light of the few lamps he would let us keep on.

I sat at the kitchen counter drinking my tea, watching him pour glasses of ice water for my sisters' Dramamine. After he put the pitcher away he stood there in his T-shirt, his arms tensing and relaxing and re-tensing with expectancy, his crew-cut temples and eyesockets lost in shadow. By the time the glasses were set up and the girls came out he would be looking out the back window at the dog pens or the overflowing garden, at anything other than us. We were nothing but background to him. Try as I might to ignore this feeling of anonymity, it passed through me like a wave of sickness as I drank. Later in the rearview I would see his eyes for the first time, and for the first time would let myself think of how lost within himself he seemed. They burned in the dusty glass with nervous readiness, the look of ambush.

We avoided the Turnpike as we traveled west. He saw the toll road as a mercenary hoax foisted on the world by the old Jewish families of Cleveland. It was a scam so obvious as to not require instruction. This made us have to detour through county after county of dry, flat tableland, keeping us from the wooded roads of the Mohican and Maumee Valleys. These were the days before air conditioning, and my sisters fidgeted as the temperature rose.

"These toll roaders are getting squeezed out," he said, "By the interstates. Going the way of the dinosaur."

My mother rolled her eyes and reached back between us to her stack of magazines. She looked out the window, snapping the pages as he talked.

"They'll be wondering why they built it soon. Jackrabbits'll be using it for a swimming pool."

Not to react was always a gamble. He could stop. He could go on. Most often he would take our silence for acceptance. On the subject of the road we really couldn't argue. His father Carl was a supervisor on the new North-South interstate linking Cleveland and Columbus. Our family had never had a hand in anything that seemed this great, this much out there in the world, and we swelled with the pride the old man felt in his state-issue truck and pressed khakis. We were ready to excuse our father's meandering as loyalty to the project.

Motels were the first things waiting for the unaccustomed traveler, the first thing to get you if you didn't watch out. In my father's larcenic cosmology, the truly damned soul would be the salesman who arrived by turnpike at a motel whose staff had never seen him before, like Livingston missing Stanley and walking in on a village of cannibals. My father knew their tricks. He knew what they had "snuck" into their rates. He wouldn't complain when he was on an expense account, but here there was a line to be drawn. And where was the line? Only he knew. There were hidden charges for pools, for color TV. As soon as you requested ice they marked it in a book and added it on at the end under something you wouldn't catch. Magic Fingers was to be avoided at all costs. It was only a humming noise, a do-nothing gizmo put together by a factory of Mexicans who were in with the motel. And it had vulgar associations, uses in "dirty stuff" we begged him, without success, to explain.

It was reasons like these that made the motel on our first night out the Town and Country in South Bend, a tiny, unprepossessing place whose management had lived in fear of him for years. Its giant neon diving woman jackknifed and straightened over the road, and my mother pointed to her each year and said how amazing it was she was still in the air. Its days were over as the Ritz of the dinner theater circuit, but still the place excited her. My father grumbled ("The money those people make? They should be shot") when she sighted one of these "stars," game show types doing summer stock or shortened operas served up in restaurants to Chicago money. Sometimes she would stop them by the pool to talk. It was always a woman with large rings and a little dog. They looked haggard, their hands shaking as they rooted in their bags.

My father scared all of us one night when one of these people had been given our table at the restaurant. We hardly ever ate there. The prices contained hidden charges they needed to keep up the pool, the uselessly doo-dadded roof of the parking structure, the crowds of silly signs that lined the drive. Usually he would buy a box of chicken we would eat in the room. But he was tired of making the run, and some special sacrifice—weathering extra miles or leaving a clean car—had earned us this evening of luxury. The sour-faced maitre'd was reminded of this as my father paced in front of the counter.

"We had a reservation," he said. The veins of his neck bulged. He stood an inch above six feet and was taller than most maitre'ds, certainly this one, who glanced back and forth at the pages of the reservation book.

The little man shook his head. A mix-up, he said, was impossible. But it had happened. And impossibility didn't excuse things for my father. Impossibility happened to other people, people who "weren't watching" or who were intended for tragedy by God, like the Bangladeshis ("Those people?" he'd said that morning, reading about their floods, "Hell, they can't win"). People who made reservations—a process so delicate and mysterious he would no more let my mother do it than read a road map—were people who planned ahead, people ready for things, people who were watching. They were the kind of people to whom the world belonged—to whom a table belonged, at the very least.

"I will see what I can do," the man said. His eye ticked with new nervousness, knowing my father had noticed his Hungarian accent. He huddled with two underlings in the doorway. Its orange curtains gave off the smell of disinfectant,

The man came back stammering, his grammar shutting down like bursting fuses. He would bring a small table from a banquet room and set it up with four chairs pronto. The table was by the kitchen, he said, but the window was open. A breeze was most pleasantly blowing.

"Why can't the show folks take the table? They put their pants on in the morning same as we do."

My father would say this anytime we spoke well of anyone outside his family or small circle of friends, but did so in a clowning way, still open to proof that there was something special about really famous people. But his voice was dead serious now. Its sly, sluggish cunning let you know he meant it. When the maitre'd turned his eyes my way I felt the floor open under me.

My mother came up from behind, stuffing a magazine in her purse.

"I'm sure we'll be fine with what you're bringing," she said, "but this has never happened before, and we do want you to know we're disappointed."

She put her hand on my father's arm. He pulled against her for a second. Below the sleeve her nail tapped the skin with a sound like wood.

We ate in silence, broken by stories about the dealers he had in this and neighboring cities. My sisters had been emptied by many a roadside vomiting, and they shoveled their food in noisily, with bulging eyes, like ravenous gypsy children. My father stared at his food or up at the wall as he talked. My mother nodded, looking over once or twice to smile at me.

From South Bend we went straight northwest, avoiding Chicago and every other city we passed. Cities to him were evil in themselves, boards and bricks of an absolute, impenetrable evil.

Their clanging, smoking mills did necessary work, but drove the life out of pastoral man, men like his father and grandfather who hunted and fished and craved the green of the leaf. Their ratlike populations were too busy struggling to be good or honest. He no more blamed them for their greed or deceit than he would blame a hungry wolf for eating a lamb.

The Great Plains stretched out before us, quilt checks of yellow grain broken here and there by vibrant forests. Much of the route was not yet interstate, and the four lane blacktop would narrow to take us through small farm villages much like our own. My sisters were constantly sick. Jill learned from Lorrie to signal by clutching her stomach and making the exaggerated gulping sound John Ford's Germans made when their throats were cut. This was my father's cue to lunge (pre seat belts) at the power brakes, and in seconds she would be out and over the road, the carpet spared. My mother would hold back her hair as she coughed softly, breaking the rhythm of the still-running engine.

Once they were finished we played travel games. My father didn't like them, and part of the reason, I had to believe, was that he was never invited to play. There were two kinds of games: roadside identification and mind reading. In the first we called out trees or cattle or cars we had learned by shape on previous trips. "Jersey!" Lorrie called at every herd, slumping as my mother explained the colors of different breeds. The second was a version of charades that could lead to a lot of jumping and shouting. The miles passed and the heat settled in as our voices rose. My father's ears got redder and redder. When his hand came up from the armrest we stopped talking. We got as far back from the front seat as we could. If I peeked between it I could see his fingers and knuckles going white where he gripped the wheel.

Where were we going? We were never really sure. He loved to hunt and fish, and though he couldn't turn the trips into all out expeditions, the kind he took his brothers on, he scouted and stalked as much as he could. Sometimes he put on camouflage and left us for hours. Nestled around our luggage were lenses and stands of game telescopes wrapped in dry cleaning bags, or bird jackets filled with empty shells and traces of down. Once in a while he would pack a pistol. When I saw its sheepskin case in the trunk he winked and put his finger on his lips.

The motels in the northern plains were less suspect than the ones farther east. The people here were different, he said. They were simpler, happier, less ambitious and less moved to small dishonesties. They were straight precisely because they had nothing to prove, because they had to be, stuck the way they were in the middle of nowhere ("East Jesus" he called every town we passed). I could see in his praise of them a knifelike sliver of spite, weaker but in a way equal to his hatred of city people—a contempt of their imprisonment by place, their not being able to help what they were.

While he was praising the motels of these honest towns he would say the same of their tourist attractions, such as they were. Usually they had clunky themes like crops or land formations. The first that comes to mind is the Corn Palace in Mitchell, South Dakota. It had red cob towers and a roof of giant yellow kernels made of sheet tin. There was a Sorghum City somewhere, and a Quarryville, I think, not far from the Badlands. He liked them because they had free admission and only charged for separate booths of genuine merchandise, like corn oil or maple syrup. They were shabby, embarrassing places, but the traveler could take or leave what they offered with no worry of being taken.

The lower category of tourist joint was more common. They had a cumulative effect on him, and a long string of them could get him fuming, mile after mile, like a goaded bull. To him they embodied every secret of the trickster and the con man, every gype and prevarication. In one respect they were out front with their phoniness, making no pretense of a connection with their surroundings. Set in the middle of Missouri, Iowa or the Dakotas, they featured exotic dinosaurs, ocean life, interplanetary traveling rocks or Spanish conquistadors. They were run, he said, by men behind hidden curtains, cornfed Wizards of Oz in tattoos and sharkskin. All had served at least some state time for larceny. To get past these places, to get beyond the point of even acknowledging the thought of stopping at one—this is what separated the seasoned man from the sucker.

He called them "You-Take-'Em Joints." A true You-Take-'Em had indicators we'd learned by heart, drilled into us in years of nervous recitations. There were giveaways like painted signs, usually red letters on white, and sloping, stenciled sentences full of misspelled words. Some would come in series and form a jingle, a question and rhymed answer just strained enough to be silly and clever at the same time. We would jump up at the first one, watching my father bristle for a comment. We leaned against one another with the pressure of guessing, a feeling that what was being said was passing others over and picking us out—and the world seemed only put there for us to unpuzzle.

When we reached the place itself he ran us through the evidence, item by item, like a quartermaster sergeant.

"Shoddy sign," I would begin.

"This place is just a bunch of trailers," Lorrie chimed in.

He smiled.

"What else?"

"There's no road there. It's just a service road or something.".

"Right. And the idea of the place? What's wrong with it?"

"I'd let the girls take the clincher."

"There's no barrier reefs in Nebraska."

"Right. And why not?"

"Because there's no ocean!" Lorrie would say, dishpan curls bouncing, her face red with having gotten it out.

My mother would look up from her magazine, smiling, watching my father's smile widen under the big reflector glasses that made him look like a bee. I was beginning to distance myself from him then, less from his opinions than from the intensity that spun so mindlessly out of them. I was afraid of it and afraid of the way it scared people, flaring up in a second and then smoking out, burning to no purpose like a string of caps. I was losing my mother's capacity to absorb and forgive it. But all that would pass when we hit the stride of one of our routines, when we needed one another to bring off the show. Something like forgiveness rose up in this unspoken happiness of mutual company, all the stronger somehow for its being heated and risen in this bubble of steel and glass, this marvelous speeding shelter of his approval.

Reptile City, we could tell, was one of the lower grade spots, by all indications a You-Take-'Em joint from the top down. Its signs were spread for miles and simply said DON'T MISS!, followed by bad pictures of lizards and snakes and the bones (sometimes human) of their hapless victims. Most looked like dirty socks with eyes and forked tongue. The last one just said YOU'RE HERE. Under it was a circle of trailers and a long tin fence blistered with rust.

We'd passed the place every year. And every year it had gotten the usual treatment. Every year we'd gone down through the list for him, one or two of us giving it some special insult. But this time was different. Somehow this year we had gotten so bored, so tired, so stifled by the flatness and heat that we were ready for anything. And anything meant anything, the formerly unthinkable. We would suspend our disbelief for some competent boa wrestling. We wanted to see the motorized jaws of the Great Commando Lizard.

What was really unthinkable, of course, was that we convinced him. We hardly even had to ask. I figured later that he probably just wanted some practice.

"There's no children's rate?" my father asked.

"Very sorry to disappoint you sir but there is not!" said the man at the booth. And we saw immediately that my father was right again; these people were exactly like he'd said. The man had a check suit so shiny it looked glazed. He wore platform shoes with alternating layers of brown and cream, like the rings in the stump of a cut tree. And his part seemed odd to us, way too far down on his head.

"You could say, sir, that we're all children here at Reptile City. We never outgrow our fascination with God's strangest and most wonderful creatures." The man spoke in a startled manner, as if something were jumping up and down in front of him. He couldn't stop blinking.

"Here you go, for five," my father said, taking a ten and a five out of his wallet. Beside the cashbox was a purple roll of cardboard tickets, one end twisting away from the knot.

"Don't worry, it's not a snake!" said the man. He laughed in a quick sputter, like a baby beginning to choke.

My father looked down at the tickets in his hand and waved us through. He looked like someone who'd had a plate of food taken out from under him. We pushed through the turnstile one by one and walked out into a room filled with wide, plywood-sided boxes.

The first had an iguana. It was laying against a board in the corner. Its scales were grey like the hair of an old dog, and it seemed too weak to move. "Poor thing," my mother said.

"Real exotic," my father said. "They probably got it in Arizona."

We walked to the next box on the other side of the room. It was scattered with what looked like large, very white round rocks. Some were smudged with handprints. My mother's face must have looked puzzled leaning over them.

"Those are the eggs," the man said.

"Eggs of what?" my father asked.

"Of the Great Commando Lizard!" the man said.

My father stepped back. "Look like rocks to me."

I knew he was right, that they were rocks, and I also realized the man was wrong about the name. I knew from a book of mine that it wasn't either of the words he used, commando or kimono, but something else, something very close to each.

"Where's the lizard?" asked my father.

"The lizard," the man said, "is sick." The hand he rested his chin in was covered with rings.

"Where at? I'll take a sick lizard for the money I paid."

"At the veterinarian," the man said. He sighed. "We're hoping," he said, raising his eyes slightly. "We're praying."

My father stood there, not saying anything. He wouldn't take his eyes off the floor. "A veterinarian for the lizard," he said. "That's rich."

I could see in his eyes how angry he was. Lorrie called them "smoking" when they got like that. My mother moved up beside him and looked around at us. She pressed his arm softly to move him forward.

There were snakes in the next room. Boys in T-shirts with blond, matted hair leaned over the bins and picked them up with sticks. They laughed when the snakes dropped, clunking on the bottoms of the bins. It was a cold, empty sound.

Some of the boys seemed to be charming or training the snakes. One would hold it on a stick while the other made swirling motions in front of its head. Some had rattles as big as their heads, and one had the rusty, flaking skin of a copperhead.

"De-fanged!" said the man when he saw me watching. "De-fanged and de-venomed!" His tongue went across his upper lip like a wiper. "Every precaution has been taken."

Another snake dropped, echoing in the bin.

"Let's move on," my father said.

In the next room the snakes were larger. But they were all milk and garter and cottonmouths, nothing we hadn't seen under somebody's lawnmower. The large ones weren't long as much as fat. All of them looked too old to move.

My father was growing angrier. He started moving faster through the rooms. Sometimes he snorted when the man said something.

The loud voice in the room we were going to sounded like our guide's, but we knew it wasn't because he was always beside us, short and breathing heavy, trying to keep up with my father. A bead curtain hung in the bright, tiled arc of the doorway. My father went through first, his big hand whipping at it as it brushed him.

There was a show going on in the room. The showman looked like the man with us but without as much hair. He stood by one of the bins wearing the same bright jacket, speaking into a small, square, neck-mounted microphone. He was holding a snake by the back of its head.

"God's strangest and most beautiful creatures!" the man with us said. Only a few people were watching his lookalike. Most of them milled around, not paying attention. An old Indian stood up close.

The snake had a rattle. It shone large and white in the room's pale light.

"Tame as a household pet," the showman said, lifting the fangs of the snake over a shot glass he brought from his vest pocket. The fangs were very small. Nothing came out. The snake's eyes were closed. We wondered if it was real.

Our guide looked up at my father, but I was afraid to. My mother kept back from him now. The sides of his face and neck were flushed pink like a baby's. His fists were clenched, and it seemed best to be outside their reach.

The showman kept pressing the snake's head. Nothing came out. One of the people watching drank from a bottle he pulled out of his coat.

My father looked around at us. I hoped that if anything happened he would do it to one of the people in the place and not to us. He was shaking his head. His pupils were milky white now, like stagnant water. He looked like he did when we burned brush at our lot on winter mornings, his skin soaking up the heat and bringing it away, prickling with it.

But he didn't do anything. He just turned and went on to the next room. And we followed him, keeping back.

It was right at the doorway that we heard the shouts. I turned around and saw the showman down on the ground. The people watching had closed in around him, but they weren't getting too close. The one that came closest was the other man, our guide, the one that looked like him. The bunch of them together watching seemed to be divided from him by a pane of glass, pressing on it but not coming through.

I went closer. The snake had its head sunk in the showman's neck just under the ear. Its body was moving.

There was no sound but my mother's footsteps coming into the doorway and her saying "Oh," very soft, just behind me. My father was there too, breathing from his running.

After a minute the man who had been drinking leaned down to the showman. He took the bottle out of his coat and hit softly at the snake, trying to shoo it. It twisted away after a couple of hits and the bottle broke.

When the man started turning blue my mother screamed. The guide bent down to him, making a choking sound as he covered his mouth. He kept his eye on the snake and reached out slowly to the showman's leg. His hand snapped up, like he'd touched an electric wire.

"Something," he said, turning around to us. "Do something."

His face was glistening. His hands brushed the showman's pantcuffs now.

"He's my brother," the man said.

Then my father's breath was gone from behind me and he was running up to them. He grabbed the broken bottle and stuck the glass in behind the snake's head. It didn't move. The Indian pulled at its body. Still nothing; the snake hung on. It lay still for a moment after they came away. Then its body moved again, as if with hunger.

My father ran back into the rooms we'd run through. I don't remember much that happened when he was gone, but I do remember my mother crying again, a sort of low moaning I felt bad I couldn't stop. I was just old enough to feel my parents' powerlessness in keeping us from the sight of evil, something really worse than evil itself. I felt it then like the chill coming in through a winter door. She seemed to have changed places with me for that moment, so that she was the child and I the adult expected to give comfort, a comfort I couldn't begin to make the motions of.

Then came the blast, and right after it the smoke and the smell of smoke, and after that the smell of powder. My father was braced against the door with both hands around the pistol I'd seen in the trunk the day before. The snake was spinning on the floor in a splash of blood, it scales falling around it through the air like feathers.

In the car later it was hard listening to my mother describe the ambulance ride to the hospital. She talked about how the showman's color came back, how the paramedic—or whatever they were called then—had made small cuts around the bite and put a rubber thimble to it, and sucked and spit the poison into a bowl that he kept remarkably still as they drove. I wasn't thinking about her making the ride, which I thought at first was a little unusual. I didn't think about all that we'd seen happen in the place. I wasn't even thinking about the showman, how happy we were that he'd made it.

At first I was thinking about the shot. I mean how clean it had been, just taking the body off and leaving the head there to die where it hung. I couldn't say that its difficulty really surprised me. I'd seen him shoot wood ducks on the wing at fifty, sometimes eighty feet or more, on grey spring mornings through budding cover. They were shots that had made the other men with us stand still a minute or two with disbelief. But this was a good shot, something amazing in itself. And it was a pistol he had used. Large bore and heavy in the hand, but still a pistol.

The girls hadn't been fazed by any of this. They stood up on the seats laughing, trying to balance themselves with the luggage straps. My mother laughed as she watched them, her hair blowing in the light and blur of the window. My father drove hard out of these last pine woods of the Dakotas.

Where were we going? I didn't really know. Once again, we just weren't sure. Somewhere in the Bighorns, some of us (for some reason) thought. My father had been mentioning them in a hushed voice before we left. The fog hung on their sides, he'd said, like long grey drapes the wind would pass through.

My sisters got worse as we climbed. When the sky began to darken we could see strange forms like stalagmites on the horizon. The girls kept going until they got giddy with the things, squealing at their colors and angles of light. Soon they had my mother going. She laughed till she was almost crying, bending over, throwing herself back.

And my father? He was laughing too, and after an hour or two of watching him I realized how different things were, how something had changed in the whole picture of him. His hands were easier on the wheel. He wasn't as hunched over. There was an ease, a calm that had come over him. He seemed to be stepping forward like my mother into my sister's laughter, letting it come down, letting it fall over him like shower water.

It wasn't as if what happened was going to make him any quieter. He was itching to talk. You could see it moving along the surface of his skin, like the far off coming of a sneeze. But somehow I knew it was more to see what was going on than to say something. And even when he did talk about the usual things—the bogus places, the highway shysters—it was in a special kind of joking way, letting us know, telling us we had to know it wasn't as serious to him now.

The fountains on the horizon wavered and faded. The setting sun was covering them over in the haze its light threw on the rising dust. Looking at the map I could see we were leaving the last of the Dakota high country, heading out through the hundreds of miles of plains that lay between us and the Rockies. My mother was looking at my father like she'd never seen anything so strange. His head was back against the headrest he said he'd never use.

"Some operation they had there," he said. This seemed to confuse my sisters at first, but then I could see the ease in their faces too, and I knew they were only deciding who should take the cue.

"They could really see you coming," said Lorrie.

"A mile off," he said. "And we let down our guard." He

laughed.

"Never again," said Jill.

"No way, Jose," said Lorrie.

My mother threw in "A fool and his money are soon parted."

It was my turn. "We were poor slobs."

When we stopped laughing nobody could think of anything to say, and after a long silence he said an old line of his: "Well, we learned." We watched the sun closing in around the cinder road ahead, and in front of it, in outline, the black, grooved steering wheel and the hands that just hours ago had held the gun.

We spent that night in a town on the state line called White Prairie, in a nearly perfect motel we watched like a hawk, just in case. After dinner in the dining room we moved over to the lounge. A Texas swing band was playing. My father bought us 7-Ups and sat us on the wide, half-circle of booth so we could watch him dance with my mother. The smoothness of his movements came back again as he twirled and dipped her, holding her for long seconds before snapping her up. Sometimes he didn't dip but just drew her close in the spin, whispering something in her ear, and in holding her there seemed to be holding all of us, telling all of us that we were safe.

The Hunter Gracchus

We could not comprehend that he had disappeared, and so we were unable to walk around with the puff-eyed, blotchy somnambulism of our mothers and fathers. "We" were my sister Jane, his brother David and his younger toddler brother Barrett. We were six and five and four and two. All deaths in our family before this had been of older people, people expected to pass away, great uncles and aunts whose friends were all gone and whose lives were a kind of middle passage into that giant, hugely populated place that yawned only darkly at the other end of existence, like the Pacific Ocean. (When we visited them they would sometimes freeze in front of us, their voices sliding downward, and would call us by the names of the dead.)

But this was the death of one of us, of a child. This was an error of God, one of the true horrors and unmendable sadnesses of the earth.

He had died of appendicitis, our cousin Dalton. Such a death was unheard of even then, in 1964, in that strange time in America between the death of the President and the Beatles' first Ed Sullivan show. His parents, my uncle Daryl and his wife Elizabeth, had been at a high school basketball tournament game in Upper Sandusky. They thought the fever they left him with was benign, fit for babysitting, nothing more than a sliver of the winter flu that had blown through the Erie Valley from the north.

His fever spiked on their last ten miles home, and Darletta, the babysitter, was stretched out on the couch with him, sweating and panicked, unable to lift the phone and call my father when my uncle Daryl burst through the door with the frozen and knowing look somehow already on his face.

They wheeled Dalton into the O.R. at 2:30 a.m., three hours after his appendix burst and sent its slowing concrete poison through his bright young blood. Clemer, our rookie family doctor who had to assist the hopeless surgeons, knew going in that nothing short of a miracle would save him. He was truly faultless himself, young Clemer, but for thirty years would take one form or another of abuse for this from various members of our family.

I knew nothing of any of the foregoing—none of us did—until my uncle pulled into our driveway and stumbled down the tiny hill of our dried-out yard and into our kitchen door. I was reading a Herter's catalog in our playroom, the shadowy flats of rifles and scopes laid out in yellow columns like phone book print. He cried with a pathetic and enormous roar, like the lion stroking his tail in the Wizard of Oz. I came out to the kitchen and watched him crumpled against my mother's wettening dress, gasping, blurting over and over again the words "We lost him." I shall never again in my life hear a sound as sad as that man crying.

Five or six hours later, in the early-darkening winter evening, my mother pulled my sisters and me against that same wet dress, running her hands up and down the bumps of our spines. When it came my turn to be hugged—the oldest and strongest, the boy, went last—I looked out from the folds to see the car bearing Betty, his mother, around the corner and up the hill of Maple Street to the tiny house that had only the day before breathed in and out with the life of her own oldest child.

"There she is," my Mother said, turning me to look at the three still heads in the Ford's rear window. "They've given her something."

How do you buy a burial suit for an eleven year old boy? This was the job of my mother, and of Mary Robb, our Kentucky neighbor and an accomplished seamstress. She'd garnered this grim work for the town's funeral directors from her early girlhood of burying miners—uncles, big brothers and Harlan County city fathers—in jackets and ties that would draw attention away from the paleness of their faces or the bruises a blast or living burial had left them with. She and my mother and father chose a tweed, a herringbone brown, the finest herringbone garment, really, that any of us had ever seen. Its angles, like on most boy's jackets, shot upward rather than downward. The pattern made a dizzying, luxuriant motion of growth on a body emptied of all its air and blood, frozen in its tiny form, this form of ending.

One of the things that mystified me so much in those days, of funeral dressing and funeral planning, was the hideous laughing my cousin David and I kept up behind the backs of our parents and our visiting aunts and uncles. Our nervous giddiness never involved poor Dalton. We had enough of a sense of decency and respect for death—if not for the dead—to keep ourselves quite clear of that. Rather, the things we did were no more than heightened, even more crazy variants of the skits and accents we used to mock our grown-ups as a matter of course.

We sharpened our grandfather Chester's crackly, feckless voice. We sweetened the clunkiness of our Uncle Buddy's hangdog gait. And, with something quite close to cruelty, we began to imitate Jana's long fits of crying, those times when her face would redden and crinkle and squeeze all its water—seemingly all of the moisture of her body—out into the dish towel she always clutched close to her apron.

When I think of those black little splintery plays, I wonder if maybe we were revenging ourselves on Dalton, whether we were flinging our ten year old spit back into the face of someone who could never return it now. Dalton had had his petty cruelties, the pompous way he'd run the tiny clubs he'd formed. You'd get called before him for almost any reason, sitting up behind his card table perched in the middle of our clubhouse tent. There'd be a small ledger open in front of him. He'd tap his pencil eraser on the crisp paper, bup bup bup bup, faster and harder if you tried to smile. He'd ask if you knew what the pencil would do, if you knew what a little pencil could do.

Really, we may only have been acting out the drama of grief, meting it out with an especially childish relish. Freud said its ceremonies were compensation for our guilt in delighting that we ourselves were not among the vanished. We had no idea where Dalton had gone. But we knew enough to know we didn't want to be there too. We were like the nightingale in Bergerac, looking down at first into the high stream it sits on, thinking that it too had fallen into the water. You're startled into a kind of happiness when you feel your own being once again, like waking from a dream, and you sometimes flap and shriek all the louder in what should be a solemn time.

So we imitated the walk of our uncle Dick Cheney, the brother of the funeral director, even as he paced the downstairs of our house explaining the things he had applied to Dalton's face, the way his hair had been brushed. We imitated our Uncle Buddy getting berated by my father for forgetting his tie. Your only goddam tie, he said, for Dalton's funeral. Your only tie.

There was one skit that I remember especially, and felt especially bad about, but which must have made for one of those releases of energy, those slow, strong sprays of dissipation.

My grandmother Jana used all manner of odd locutions when she spoke, especially when she was angry. But she didn't have to be for us to hear them. "Red" was a verb that meant to clean, as in "red up the table." When we were running around her she told us constantly to "mind," an iron order hanging out in the air with no word for its referent, barked straight out from her flour-stained face. "Fast" meant mired or fastened or stuck, a state she seemed to wish on all the world when it got going around her too quickly.

On the day before the funeral, when we were trying on our own suits at her house, we'd tear away our snap-on ties, unbutton our shirts. We had seen some show on Indian tigers or Jim Doney's "Adventure Road," and David and I, enlisting even the innocent Barrett, started to claw at the couches and chairs and the waffled cushion of the deacon's bench in her dining room.

She came at us from the downstairs bathroom in a rage, telling us to stop, that we were acting like animals. She said that our nails would get caught in the fabric, that we'd be stuck fast and have to be cut away.

We took off on this for hours afterwards, each taking turns as the taciturn Jana. We forced one another into chairs, the pushed one clawing and grimacing, purse-mouthed, flailing back at the pusher's stiffening hands. We laughed as loud as we could and shouted our lines so we were sure that she could hear us.

But she wouldn't come back in, knowing we were finally dressed. She was busy herself with prayers and face powders, with fastening the latch of the bracelet that had each of our names, even Dalton's, on a flat chrome heart that jangled when she passed.

It was a sort of standoff, the four of us scrunched up like bats in the hallway's dark, the quickening blasts of laughter, the way our bodies glowed now with exhaustion where we were slumped along the wall. All of this combined in me into a shivering, ice-like guilt, the feeling of a cloud grown up in my chest that would never leave, and would always make me sick. I knew we had wronged her. I knew what vandals we had been. It was the beginning, I suppose, of my grown-up consciousness of wrongdoing, its claw-like pinchers wrapping around the heart like setting hooks around a diamond solitaire.

Still, in the middle of all this I began to miss him, and as the evening lengthened I found I wasn't alone in having the visitation of this feeling. David and I had planned to sprinkle some pond water on him in his open coffin. Dalton had led us from one clump of open springs to the next in the farm country around our homes, gathering frogs eggs and crawfish and wounded birds we would find a way to nurse back into their branches. We felt we owed him this gesture, this wild gratitude, like the Wyandots who'd lived here once would owe a blood remembrance to their hunting scouts.

But there was something else about the pond water. Dalton was going somewhere none of us had ever been before. We were curious about things he might take with him and wondering if we could help him gather them together, and in that way give him something of ourselves to take along. Maybe, in that same sense, we could also be there with him even though we weren't with him, the way friends of Egyptians stayed in the tombs in streams of colored cloaks and cats and polished stones.

So after the short sermon in the quiet, shaded, almost unbelievable thickness of the flowers' smell, and after watching Jana hunched and jerking with her tears, which made me feel like a monster all over again, and after Reverend Chapin had shut his book and the cousins and uncles from out of town that we really didn't know had filed out, it was time for all of us to go up one by one and say goodbye, before Betty and Uncle Daryl would be all alone with him in the parlor for whatever would happen then.

David and Barrett and the other boy cousins had made me go last. Being oldest (after Dalton), I had been given the job of sprinkling the water, which somebody had put in a palm-sized, emptied plastic bottle of dishwashing liquid. I put it in the deep right pocket of my strange new suit. It was heavy, but I couldn't feel the water move.

As soon as I got the courage to get up and start moving, my mother pressed my back gently from her chair and I passed her and my father. I went up and looked in.

The shadow of the lid fell across the jacket and his jacketed breast like the half-angle of a coat of arms. But his face was sunny, his skin amazingly fresh and bright. At first it looked as gold and smooth and unfreckled as a yellow apple. The front of his brush cut was tufted and soft, and seemed to give and take under my breath as if it had just been washed and was full of static electricity.

His mouth was straight, the same way it was when he was talking about what the pencil could do, and his lips were creased with a stick or a paste that was colored like flesh.

I brought the bottle out and cupped it under my hands as I leaned them just over the edge of the polished bronze. I unscrewed the cap and put my finger in until it reached the middle knuckle.

The cold down in my chest, still there after all our laughing, still there after all those days, was lifting now, and something else was following it in. I thought how even in the coldest mornings in the fields the ground heat came, the sun's warmth filling the grass between the ponds he had led us to. You felt it come quickly, then weakly, then quickly again, like the waves of gas heat coming up out of a floor register.

I lifted my finger out of the bottle and held it in the air for a minute until a drop came down, watching my finger and the fingers of his own hands. The color of the skin there was darker than his face, like the brownest part of a buckeye or the broad pond banks you could see from all sides as you stood in some place on the hills above them.

It was his hands I looked at now, only his hands. They were twisted and curled from the palms to the tips, like the vines I imagined the diggers' shovels would have to break through in this cold March ground. They were clutched so tight against the blankets, holding on to the ground of all of us—not ready to be cut, not ready to let go.

The author wishes to acknowledge the editors of the following publications, in which these stories, some in an earlier form, first appeared:

1. *Indiana Review*: "White Prairie"
2. *Descant*: "Ophelia"
3: *Santa Monica Review*: "Mimesis"; "The Branch"; "Flashbox"; "Tyumen Is My Dwelling Place"
4. *Pushcart Prize: Best American Stories 2022*: "Flashbox"
5. *Louisiana Review*: "Hard Times"
6. *El Portal*: "Rain In The Heart"
7. *Juked*: "Flatlanders"; "The Baby"
8. *Texas Review*: "Summer's Blood"
9. *Transformation*: "Green, Whale-Back Mountain"
10. *Fiction*: "The Branch (titled 'Pindar')"
11. *Pacific Review*: "The Farmer Wears the Crown of Thorns"

"Property" is for Colm Tóibín, who gave me its first line.
"Tyumen is My Dwelling Place" borrows its basic form from David Malouf's classic story "Closer." The author wishes to thank Mr. Malouf and his agents at Coleridge, White.
"The Baby" is modeled on a chapter of David Szalay's novel, *Turbulence*.
"The Wave Function" borrows ideas from Joyce Carol Oates' story, "The Radio Astronomer".

First Readers and Facilitators:

Los Angeles: Deborah Bauman; Maya, Amelia and Evan Wirick; Anthony Robinson; Dean Ferguson; Raifort Rogers; Eric Berkowitz.

New York: John Rounds; Joseph Sieger; Ann Schirrmeister; the late Andrew Schirrmeister; Erin Hosier, my American agent at Dunow Carlson; Laura Mazer; Denise Oswald; David & Katie Katz; Frank Boesch and Stephanie Secolsky; Mark Mirsky.

Dallas: Jane Drake; Anthony Robison and Beacon Editorial; Professors Jon Sands and Thomas Pitts; the staff at Descant (Ft. Worth), Dr. Kenneth Dekleva.

Yale: Sophie Pollack, Chip Marvin.

London: Malu Halasa (from whom all blessings come); Andy Cox; Mitch Albert; Jo Glanville; Maria Porzkova at BBC-Warsaw; Judith Herman at BBC Oxford; Rose George; Masoud Golshorki; Caroline Issa; the staff at Soho House.

For support: The late Paul Ruffin and the staff at *Texas Review*; George Garrett at U.Va.; the staff at *Quarterly West* and *Santa Monica Review*; Jim Kearns; Paul Sandberg; Robert Phillips at U.Va.; Brady Unruh; Charlie Yu; Lee Abbott; David Mamet; Carrie Malcolm; Ethan Hawke.

The Editors: Andrew Tonkovitch; Richard Olafson; Geoffrey Wolff; Lanie Perlman; Janet Stone Herman; S.L. Wisenberg; Sophie Pollack.

www.ingramcontent.com/pod-product-compliance
Lightning Source LLC
Chambersburg PA
CBHW030521310726
48979CB00010B/1754/J

9781771715683